ASSAULTED SOULS

A post-apocalyptic tale of an epic struggle for survival in a decimated wasteland.

by

William Blackwell

ACKNOWLEDGEMENTS

Heartfelt thanks to my loyal and supportive friends and
family, the hardworking staff at
Telemachus Press, and Winslow Eliot. Special thanks to the
Government of Prince Edward Island for its financial support.

To Katie, you are an inspiration.

I will show you fear in a handful of dust.
–T.S. Eliot, *The Wasteland*

ASSAULTED SOULS

Chapter One

"Where am I?"

"You're in a hole."

"I know, but where am I? Where's the hole?"

"You don't know? How many times do I have to tell you?"

"Would you mind telling me again?"

"You're on Earth, or what's left of it."

"What's Earth?"

"Do I have to tell you again?"

"Would you mind?"

"Earth is our planet. It's where we were born, where we live. That is, until the bomb was dropped. Now everything's fucked up."

"Who am I?"

"Listen, I'm not going to do this again. You ask the same questions every day. I'm sick of it. I'm leaving."

"Please tell me who I am and I won't bother you anymore."

"You're Nathan King."

Nathan King looked at the skinny, partially-clad man squatting in front of him, illuminated faintly by the flickering flame from the small, white candle, and wondered who he was. His greasy long hair pointed out at odd angles and, but for a ripped pair of denim shorts, nothing else covered his body, except black dirt smears across his chest, legs, and face. Lines creased his weathered face, more pronounced on his furrowed brow. The corners of his lips pointed down, the signs of much suffering etched into his worn features.

They sat cross-legged around the candle, the only light and heat source in the otherwise dark and dank-smelling cave.

"Who are you?" Nathan asked.

"When are you going to start remembering shit?" the man snarled.

"I don't know." *I can't remember one day to the next.* "But if you tell me I'll stop bothering you."

"You said that before."

"Did I?"

"Yeah."

"Okay, this time I mean it. Please tell me who you are?"

A long pause. The only sound was the faint howling of the wind, increasing in intensity, far above them on the surface of the Earth.

"I'm Edward Sole, your friend."

"You're my friend?"

"Didn't I just say that?"

"Yeah, you did."

Funny, I don't remember him. Or is it? I don't seem to remember much else. Should I ask him how long we've been down here? No, better not. Enough for one day. "What do you want to do now?"

"Not much we can do now. It's getting late. I'm going to bed. You should do the same." Edward extracted a small candle from his pocket, lit it on the communal candle, stood up eyeing Nathan despairingly. "We should try and get some clothes tomorrow and some food. As long as the Neanderthals don't return." He disappeared down a cavernous passage.

Nathan looked around, trying to make sense of his surroundings. But the cave, dimly lit by the flickering candle, was mostly black. *Neanderthals? Where's my bed? I'm hungry.*

He absently put his hand to his aching stomach, realizing for the first time he didn't have a shirt either and he could feel his ribs. He examined his stomach, his arms and legs, saw the same black dirt smears and frowned. His only clothing, a knee-length pair of cotton shorts with multiple pockets. *Travel shorts.* He could barely tell they might have been green at one time but were now mostly black and brown with dirt and grime.

I smell bad, he thought, bringing his nose down to his hairy armpit. He brought his hand to his face, felt the scruff of a thick beard. *Did I have this before?* He ran his hands through his hair and realized it was long, disheveled, and greasy. *Like what's-his-name.*

"What happened?" he asked out loud, his voice echoing through the cave. He strained to try and remember. He sat a long time in silence but very little entered his distressed mind. At least, not anything that would remind him of where he was and how he got here. *How could this be? I'm here with that guy in this dark and desolate place and can't remember anything. Please, please mind, remember something, anything.*

But still nothing came to him and he shivered, wondering if it was more from the cold or from his fear. Fear that he would never remember anything, would continue to ask that guy—*what was his name again?*—the same questions over and over again, every day. That would suck big time.

His stomach growled, breaking the long silence, and he flinched, rubbing his arms which were now crawling with goose bumps. *Remember something. Anything. Travel shorts. You like to travel. That's something. Yeah, but not enough. Travel where? And when?*

He felt overwhelming sadness rise up from inside his heart and penetrate the depths of his soul. He leaned his head into his hands and started crying. He couldn't stop it if he wanted to. The sobs started weakly, a whimper, and slowly grew in volume, the tears streaming down his face until he sat wracked with sobs, his head buried in his hands, tears running down his hands, arms, threatening to extinguish his only source of light and heat.

Finally the sobs ebbed in intensity, were reduced to a whimper again and gradually subsided. *I'm running out of tears. Stop crying, you baby. Edward's going to think you're a little wimp. Wait. Edward.*

"I remembered his name." Nathan tried to smile, but was too weak, cold and hungry. He slowly picked up the candle and stood up. He turned around, trying to figure out where he might sleep. *Should I go where Edward went?*

Before he could answer the question, the small flame illumed an oval-shaped opening in what now appeared to be a network of caves. He walked into it holding the candle, noticing the ground was strewn with garbage. He accidentally kicked a tin can and it bounced off the rock walls ahead of him—cling, clang, cling, clang—before it finally stopped and the tunnel became quiet again.

After about thirty feet, walking crouched down to avoid bumping his head, the tunnel led into another much larger cave with a vast ceiling, indiscernible in the dim light. He glanced around, trying to find his bearings, having no idea where he was or what he might find.

A scuffling sound near his feet made him leap up in fright and he smacked his head on the low stone above. He looked down and saw small glowing yellow eyes regarding him. *That's a rat. There, you remembered something else.* The rat stopped, eyeing him curiously for a few seconds before slowly crawling away into the blackness. The rat was not afraid. *Do I know him? Why is he not afraid of me?*

He held the candle in front of him, searching the cave for a place to sleep. His body had begun to tremble with fear or cold, he no longer knew which. Then he saw it, a clump of sleeping bags and blankets, a worn pillow, off in a corner on a tattered mattress. He walked over, knelt down, perching the candle precariously between some rocks and climbed into bed. Mattress springs poked into his back and he rearranged some of the blankets to try and take the edge off. It helped, but only a little.

He twisted and turned, pulling a sleeping bag over his head until he finally curled up and was still. *What about the candle? Can't sleep with that on.*

He blew it out and listened. He could hear the shuffling of the rat, the whistling of the cold wind. *Will I have to eat the rat or is he my friend too?* he thought, scratching his aching belly. He closed his eyes and his mind raced. About an hour later, overcome with fatigue, he finally felt sleep taking hold. Only one thought lingered, moments before he drifted off: *How am I ever going to survive in this wasteland?*

Chapter Two

"Do you want to survive?"

"Yeah," Nathan whispered.

"Well, then you've got to kill him," Edward said softly. "We need food."

They were above ground the next day, perched behind a stump of what was once a very large tree. The surrounding landscape was barren and sand-colored, the sky an orange haze of thin clouds, the sun behind the clouds glowing reddish-orange. Small outcrops of debris punctuated the otherwise desolate landscape.

Nathan held a crossbow, Edward at his side instructing him on technique. "Here, you pull it back slowly, once you reach this point let go, but hold it steady, make sure you have him in your sights before you let go."

Nathan flinched as he eyed the small camouflaged rabbit, only spots of white revealing its identity. Otherwise, it was the beige color of sand and blended in almost perfectly with the hostile landscape. He leveled the crossbow, lined up the rabbit head in his sights, and released the arrow. But his right arm moved just slightly during release and the arrow narrowly missed the small prey, which raised its eyes immediately and darted away after identifying its predators.

"Give it to me," Edward said, snatching the crossbow from his hands impatiently. "We'll never eat if I leave it up to you." He stood up and walked toward an outcrop of debris far away in the distance.

"Where are you going?" Nathan asked, catching up and walking a few feet behind him.

"We need clothing. And food." Pointing to the debris pile. "Over there, let's see what we can find."

Nathan followed and they walked along in silence for a few minutes, like a couple of primitive men in search of food and clothing.

"Edward," Nathan finally said.

Edward looked at him in surprise. "You remembered my name?"

"Yeah."

"You can call me Ed if you like, but if you can't remember then Edward's fine."

"Okay, Edward."

A few minutes later they arrived at the debris pile, its contents slowly coming into focus. It had once been a house on what looked like a farmstead. Large log beams jutted out at abnormal angles, the remnants of an asphalt shingle roof precariously perched atop the pile. Bits of metal, clothing, household items, furniture, and damaged appliances also rendered its twisted mass.

Nathan sat down on a tree stump as they surveyed the fractured monument to a better life. Ed rummaged through the contents. He found a few garbage bags of clothing and groped through them. He pulled out a white t-shirt, smelled it, and put it on. He found another long-sleeve button up shirt with a collar and put that over the t-shirt. Finally he dug out a tattered blue parka with a furry hood and put it on.

"Well aren't you going to look for some clothes?" he finally asked Nathan. "It gets awfully cold at night around here. You're going to need them."

Nathan had his face in his hands and was just starting to become overcome with sadness again. He looked at his friend. "Okay," he said, slowly getting up and walking over to the pile.

A few minutes later, Nathan was dressed in tattered hiking boots, a rather good pair of blue jeans, layered shirts, a kangaroo jacket, and a red jacket, the style clearly denoting the feminine gender. He also wore a black baseball cap with the red word Budweiser screen-printed on it.

"Shhhhh," Ed said, bringing his index finger to his lips. He pointed left and Nathan saw another rabbit perched about thirty feet away, crouched behind an old wooden crate. The wind had picked up and the rabbit's fur fluttered in the distance.

Ed picked up the crossbow, container of arrows, crouching down behind an old metal garbage can and took aim. Nathan had frozen to the spot, watching. He had to admit his stomach was still knotted with hunger and when he'd gotten up this morning he had even done a little searching for the one rat he had seen crawling around. He had planned on eating the rat but couldn't find it.

Ed released the arrow and the crossbow twanged, the only sound but for the faint wailing of the wind. It whizzed through the air and found its mark, penetrating the rabbit's head. The animal hopped two or three steps, slumped over spasmodically twitching for a few seconds before dying.

Ed smiled, revealing brown and black stained teeth. "Dinner." He approached his kill. "Let's go to the cave and eat. We don't have much time."

Ed picked up a cardboard box, threw some items into it along with the dead rabbit, and handed Nathan a worn-out knapsack that he had also packed with items. "Here. Carry this."

"What's in it?"

"Some food. And cutlery."

Nathan thought of asking why they didn't have much time, but quickly changed his mind. The afternoon had been going well with Ed and he didn't want to ruin it. He had strained his mind all day trying to put pieces of his past together. But not much would come to him. He vaguely remembered a life in a civilization much more modern than where he was stuck right now but it was an unsolved puzzle and Nathan didn't know if he had consciously blocked the memories or they had disappeared as the result of some major traumatic event. He didn't want to think about it right now anyway. He was starving and wanted to eat.

About twenty minutes later, they arrived at the mouth of the cave, where a few piles of wood and debris were scattered to the side of a makeshift fire pit surrounded by odd-sized rocks. Using some tiny twigs, a few bits of paper, and a lighter, Ed quickly had a small fire blazing. They sat cross-legged around it. Ed reached into the knapsack, pulled out a large carving knife, held it over the fire momentarily, and started skinning the animal.

When he was finished, he found a large branch, carved it into a spear, impaled the rabbit and held it over the fire, rotating it every few minutes.

"Do we have anything to drink?" Nathan asked, his throat was parched with dust and starting to ache.

Ed fumbled around in the knapsack, finally fishing out two cans of Coke and handing one to him.

He watched Ed pop the cap off, smother his mouth to the opening as the can fizzed up in his face, before he copied the movements. The liquid tasted sweet and fizzy and Nathan finished three quarters of the contents in two long gulps. He studied the red can. *Coke. I've had this before. Where?*

A little while later, they sat quietly eating barbequed rabbit from makeshift cardboard plates, cut out of the side of a cardboard box. Ed eyed his knife collection, an acquisition from the debris pile. He picked a long machete-style implement up, brandishing it with a side-to-side swinging motion before skewering a cooked piece of meat and biting into it.

"You should get familiar with one of these," he said, tossing Nathan a large serrated edge carving knife. It skidded across the ground and came to a stop a few inches from his crossed leg. "It might save your life."

"What's there to be afraid of?" Nathan asked, picking it up and stabbing it into his portion of meat. He lifted it to his mouth, ravenously biting off large chunks.

"I told you. The Neanderthals."

"Who are they?"

"They're a violent tribe who rape, pillage, and steal. It's survival of the fittest, literally, buddy. And you don't look very fit."

"Neither do you," Nathan said to a gaunt face, indistinctly illuminated by the flickering flames.

The orange sky was getting darker, the crimson sun setting in the distance. They looked out at the open plain, desolate but for the odd mound of debris haphazardly scattered. The wind moaned, the temperature dropped.

"Yeah, but I know how to defend myself," Ed said. "Who do you think got you here?"

"I don't know. I can't remember."

"It was me. I dragged you here just before the bomb was dropped."

"How long have we been here?"

"Three months and thirteen days."

"How do you know?"

"I mark the days on the wall."

"Oh. So has the whole world been destroyed?"

"I don't know. No communication."

"Where are we?"

Ed was growing impatient again. "I already told you. Do we ..."

"No, I mean what city, what country are we in? I'm starting to remember a few things."

"We're in rural Prince Edward Island, somewhere near Montague."

"Oh." Nathan paused a few minutes, finishing the last delicious morsel of his rabbit and licking the bones clean. He tossed a few bones into the fire and stared at Ed. *Who is he?* "What year is it?"

"It's July 16, 2016," Ed said, tossing a few bones into the fire, picking up his machete and standing. "We should go back into the cave."

"What for?" Nathan said, enjoying the orange sky, even though it had hurt his eyes for the first half hour or so. He knew he hadn't seen real brightness in a very long time, even if it was an eerie orange post-apocalyptic sunset.

"I told you," Ed snarled. "It's danger ..."

A large rock whizzed past Edward's head, narrowly missing him. As he spun around, brandishing the machete to face his attacker, another one cracked him square in the forehead.

"Fuck," he said staggering, falling to the ground inches from the small blaze. "Neanderthal—get him!"

In the twilight, Nathan could barely discern the image charging forward, wielding a large crudely fashioned club. He looked almost ape-like, grizzled with a full beard, covered in animal furs, mouth wide open, shouting indecipherable babble.

His heart racing with adrenaline, Nathan quickly grabbed his carving knife, waving it at the attacker. He ducked as the swinging bat whooshed passed his head and connected with a rock outcrop with a loud crack.

The Neanderthal growled and advanced forward, swinging. Nathan ducked again, simultaneously reaching out with a slashing motion, cutting into the attacker's leg. The Neanderthal stepped back for a second, surveying the dripping blood, and attacked again with angry resolve.

Nathan stepped back, slamming into the rock wall as the bat came down on him. It was all he could do to dive to the ground, narrowly avoiding a crushed skull. He instinctively rolled as the bat came down again and connected with the dirt a few inches away.

"Aaaaaahhh," the Neanderthal said, spinning around.

Ed had staggered to his feet and accurately thrown one of the blades, which had lodged in the predator's back.

"He's coming for me," Ed said. "Get him!"

Nathan got to his feet and in an instant leaped on the attacker's back. *I don't know if I have the strength for this.* In a swift motion, as the Neanderthal swung him around, he put blade to throat and sliced with what little strength he had left. He heard the hissing and gurgling sound of air and blood discharging from a severed esophagus, felt the gush of warm blood soaking his hands as the predator fell forward into the fire, Nathan still clinging to his back.

Ed was already running for the cave entrance. "Let's go. There'll be more."

Nathan thought he would collapse with fatigue and fall back into the fire but he forced himself to stagger after Ed. They arrived at a large steel door and Ed produced a skeleton key, opened it, and they went inside.

"You did good," Ed said, securely locking the door behind him, fishing into the knapsack and producing a small LED flashlight, which he turned on. He pointed the beam to his forehead and Nathan could see the small cut trickling blood into his eye, down his nose.

"How's it look?" Ed asked.

"It doesn't look that deep. Do we have anything to clean it?"

"In the cave. Some alcohol, I think."

Someone banged on the door loudly.

"Shit, they're trying to get in," Nathan tensed. "Can they get in?"

"No, they'll go away soon. It's going to get real cold at nightfall. Nuclear winter, I think it's called. Let's go."

Ed led and Nathan followed down a long, winding tunnel, just tall and wide enough to walk without crouching. The thumping and growling grew faint.

After a few minutes they reached an opening, their ritualistic meeting ground where they had conversed previously before departing to their respective sleeping quarters.

"Do you have another one of those?" Nathan asked, pointing to the flashlight as he panted for breath.

"It's a flashlight. And no, I don't." Ed shone the beam to the ground, locating a cardboard box of candles. "Take one of those."

Nathan picked up a candle and Ed produced his lighter and lit it. He picked up a garbage bag, rummaged through it, finally pulling out a bottle of rubbing alcohol and a white cloth. "Could you help me?" he said, handing Nathan the bottle and sitting on the ground.

Nathan sat down beside him, opened the bottle and poured some of the liquid on his temple, quickly wiping it clean with the white cloth. Ed took the cloth and held it to his head.

"Thanks," he said. After a short pause, "I'm going to bed. We need to make a plan tomorrow. We won't last long like this."

Nathan nodded. He was physically and mentally spent, and the image of his dirty bed linens and old mattress on the debris-strewn ground sounded more appealing than anything he could think of right now.

They went their separate ways.

Nestled in his dirty sleeping bag, the candle perched a few feet away hazily illuming the surrounding squalor, Nathan reached into his pocket and produced a bite-sized morsel of barbequed rabbit.

The rat squeaked, scurrying up to the candle, tempted by the scent. Its yellow eyes stared at him, unflinching, unblinking.

He put the piece of meat down by the candle. The rat quickly gripped it with its small teeth and darted away.

The last image in his mind before drifting off was of a shapely blonde woman, bound and gagged, partially clad and wide-eyed with fear.

Chapter Three

In a makeshift fortress ten feet below ground and about a mile across the barren windswept plain, Cadence Whitaker, wide-eyed and trembling with fear, watched her captor descend the rickety stairs, wondering grimly what he would do next.

Thorvald, a beefy man with grey matted hair and an oversized unkempt beard, had visited her about an hour earlier threatening to kill her if she didn't reveal the whereabouts of her boyfriend, Nathan.

She had kept her mouth shut and it had cost her. "Nod when you're ready to talk," he had said, sliding his meaty paws across her stomach, smiling as his hand slid across her pubic mound, covered only by white lace panties. His hand had roamed up to her white bra, cupping one full breast before she had finally grunted and nodded.

Thorvald had removed the cloth gagging her mouth and panic-stricken, she had told him she would reveal the location of Nathan if he would give her a glass of water. Her throat was parched and ached from thirst.

Tied spread-eagle on an old mattress, she eyed the glass of water now as he lowered it to her lips. He slowly drained the contents into her gulping mouth. It was cold, wet and refreshing and she coughed on the last mouthful, too thirsty and swallowing too fast, a small stream dribbling down her chin and neck.

"You talk now," he said, tossing the glass into an improvised wooden wall where it shattered. He sat down cross-legged and touched her arm, slowly sliding it up to her armpit. His arm was scabbed with sores and a few of the red blisters also scarred his cheeks and forehead.

She shuddered. *Do I know where Nathan is? Even if I did, would I tell this monster? I have to say something, or he'll assault me. But even if I don't, he'll assault me. Damned if I do, damned if I don't.*

"I only know the general direction," she said. "We got separated before the blast. I never got to see the bunker."

"Tell me what direction."

"Take your fucking hand off me or I won't tell you anything."

Thorvald removed his grimy hand and grunted. "Where?"

She glanced around the ramshackle room, listening to the shack creak as the wind's intensity increased. "I can't tell from down here. I need to be topside."

There was a moment's pause. "I can't take you topside tonight. It's getting ugly out there."

Cadence knew roughly where the cave was but she was buying time, stalling for a chance to get topside and maybe escape with her life. For the last three months, she had survived in a dry well about forty feet below the surface. She had rushed down just before the blast with some boxes of canned goods, sleeping bags, water and a small flashlight. She had survived on the food, too afraid to go to the surface for fear of radiation exposure. But, during the last week, she had taken to killing and eating her rat roommates after initially fattening them with food morsels. And her water supply had run dry so she had popped her head out, straining to push the boulders she had rolled over the well hole.

It was then that Thorvald Reskie had spotted and kidnapped her. He had said that Ed and Nathan had anticipated the nuclear disaster and built a bomb shelter, inviting only a few close friends and family. He also knew many of their family members had died during the blast. He had been feeding on some of them and a pile of bones, a macabre symbol of his enormous appetite, were piled about three feet high in a corner of the room. But Thorvald was running out of corpses to eat and wanted to see what, if any, food remained at the bomb shelter. He had also heard it was much more secure than his ersatz abode and he needed something better to protect him from the marauding Neanderthals. He had seen them kill on the surface before and knew it was only a matter of time before they captured and killed him. What Thorvald didn't yet realize was that he was suffering from severe radiation exposure and only had another two or so months to live. The radiation had already infected his mind, producing a stark raving lunatic.

Looking at the bones grimly, Cadence believed it was only a matter of time before he raped, killed, and ate her.

But Thorvald believes Nathan is alive and living in the bomb shelter. Nathan mentioned the bomb shelter. But how does he know about the shelter or that Nathan is alive?

Her loyal boyfriend of five years had fallen off the roof of their rural oceanfront home in PEI a few days prior to the end of the world and had suffered terrible amnesia. After being released from hospital, he had no idea who anyone was, including himself.

A few days later, he had wandered off in the middle of the night and she had never heard from him again. A police and civilian search had netted nothing.

"Let's go topside tomorrow and I'll tell you where it is." And then after a pause. "I'll show it to you."

"You better," he said, waving to the bone collection. "Unless you want to end up like them."

"I thought you said they were already dead when you ate them." She didn't know what else to say.

"Yeah, but I'm getting hungry."

She wanted to take his mind off his hunger with the promise of a good meal. She would do almost anything *not* to be his next meal. "I know they have lots of food at the shelter, enough for a year. But, it might have been invaded already by the Neanderthals, as you call them. Nathan might already be dead."

"I don't think so," he said, reaching for a sawed-off shotgun leaning against a wall. He picked it up, cocking it open to verify it was loaded. Two red shell casings were visible and he closed it again.

"How do you know?" she asked, getting nervous at the sight of the gun.

"I shot one yesterday, blew his brains out. Before I killed him, he told me he saw Nathan on the open plain with Ed, foraging for supplies."

Her heart skipped a beat. *Thank God. He's alive.* "He didn't tell you where the shelter is?"

"No."

Good. I've got an ace in the hole. "Well, you get me a blanket, another glass of water, I'll take you to the shelter tomorrow. But you so much as lay another hand on me, you're going to have to kill me, because I won't tell you shit. And the

Neanderthals will come for you, slice you open and eat you for breakfast."

Chapter Four

"What're we eating for breakfast?" Russ Wiseman asked Karl Mulligan the next morning as they sat around a pock-marked table in a debris-laden basement room twenty feet below the Earth's surface.

Five other motley men sat on two couches in a corner of the room. Some played cards and others chatted.

"How the fuck should I know?" Karl snapped. "Look around. I think there's some cans in the back." Karl wasn't in a very good mood that morning. You could say that someone had shit in his cornflakes but he had run out of cornflakes yesterday, so that wouldn't be quite accurate. In fact, the Neanderthals, a rag-tag group of raping, pillaging murderers, had run out of a lot of things lately. A group of criminals who had escaped a maximum security prison just outside of Halifax, they had stolen a boat and made their way to PEI a few months after the nuclear holocaust, believing the island would be much easier to exploit. They had fashioned an opportunistic existence in the basement of a former hospital in Montague, just outside the immediate blast zone.

They went on daily raids for survival and often killed just for the fun of it. Although, in Karl's mind, he had been given a new lease on life, but it wasn't exactly the kind of life he had in mind. He had dreamed of something far more luxurious than the cluttered dungeon of what was once a modern hospital. But still, he had to admit, it was much better than doing life in a maximum security penitentiary without the chance for parole.

He wasn't a very nice man. In a rage, he had shot and killed his wife and two small kids. Why? Because they were making too much noise while he was trying to concentrate on his war video game, *Metro 2033*. The self-appointed leader of the Neanderthals, he hated people who didn't let him concentrate.

He studied the map on the table, trying to discern the location of where Theo, a gang member, had recently been killed; the second in a matter of weeks. His throat had been slashed and Russ, second in command, had recently discovered his charred and bloody body smoldering in a small fire pit. The only problem was dim-witted Russ couldn't remember the location of the shelter. He claimed a windstorm had blown in shortly after the discovery and had impaired his ability to pinpoint it.

"Do we have any cornflakes?" Russ asked, getting up and walking toward a small pantry at the back of the room.

"I fucking told you yesterday we ran out of cornflakes," Karl said. "Are you trying to fuck with me while I'm concentrating?"

Russ knew better than to tempt fate. That much, he did remember. "No. Sorry."

Karl studied the map while Russ returned with a can of beans, popped the top off, sat down, and began spooning the mixture into his mouth.

Karl pounded his massive fist on the table and glared at Russ, pulling the map over to him. "You mean to tell me it's south of Montague and you don't know where or how far?"

Russ started at the outburst, spilling some of the beans on the tattered map. He wiped them off quickly and studied the map again. He hadn't got off to a very good start this morning with the behemoth of a man sitting in front of him, and he hoped to change that real soon.

"I think it's somewhere around there," he finally said, pointing to a spot on the map around Murray River.

"Are you sure?" Karl asked, his eyes narrowing.

"Pretty sure."

"I don't want to hear pretty sure. I want to hear sure," Karl said, angrily regarding the tall skinny man with the goatee eating beans.

"I have some good news," Russ said, smiling a rotten-tooth smile.

"What's that?" Karl asked, scratching his thick red beard.

"The other truck broke down. Most of the electrical is fried in the vehicles we do find, but I found one that's been preserved. And I found some gas. I think we can get it going."

The one thing, possibly the only thing Karl liked about Russ, a serial pedophile, was his mechanical inclination. He might have killed him a long time ago if it wasn't for that. Serial pedophiles don't do well in prison, any prison. And they certainly don't do well in the general population, especially one without law and order.

Karl smiled, exposing a perfect pair of dentures. In his late fifties, he long ago had his rotten teeth pulled and replaced with dentures. He didn't like foul mouths.

"Good," he said. "That *is* good news. Now let's get that fucking beast running and let's go spear us some Neanderthal killers."

Chapter Five

"Fuck," Thorvald said, reaching for the handsaw again as he smeared blood on his camouflaged military fatigues. He was sawing the leg off the Neanderthal he had killed a few days ago and the bone was giving him some trouble. It didn't help that the saw blade had dulled considerably, the result of overuse and lack of maintenance.

He had thought, once he got part way through, that he could just snap the leg off, but the bone, like a half-cut tree branch clinging on to the bitter end, just wouldn't snap. He had contemplated biting into raw flesh but had tried that once. He hadn't acquired a taste for human flesh unless it was barbequed on an open flame.

He grunted, resuming his back and forth motion with the saw. Breathing deeply, beads of sweat dropping from his furrowed brow, he finally heard a snapping motion and grinned.

"There you go, you little fuck," he said, slinging the leg over his shoulder, grabbing his shotgun and walking towards a small fire he had started next to his decrepit basement suite.

Arriving at the blaze, he set the leg down and reached for a rod iron spear he had fashioned. He impaled the leg, positioning it slightly above the blaze on two large boulders. It was a homemade rotisserie.

He sat down on a log stump next to the fire, savoring the sweet smell of burning flesh and picking at a dime-sized scab on his arm that had started bleeding. He would eat first and then go on a hunting expedition with Cadence. He didn't like hunting on an empty stomach. And, although he had thought of inviting her to dinner, his twisted mind reasoned she had not yet developed a taste for human flesh, barbequed on an open flame or raw for that matter. *That would take time.*

He stood, poked at the flames, and tossed another log into the blaze. The wind swirled, blowing black smoke into his face, eyes, and lungs. He coughed a few times, finally spitting a blood-soaked mucous ball into the fire.

Cadence shivered on the small mattress, tugging at the zip-ties binding her arms. It was no use. She couldn't break the strong plastic. It only tightened further, digging into her flesh, marking it red and purple.

Her arms and legs ached and her stomach was knotted with hunger pangs. *When's he coming down? I'm going to fix him.* Her story had bought her a little time unmolested. Last night Thorvald had sat next to her behaving himself and trying to engage her in conversation. She had resisted initially but then decided she would have a much better chance at survival if she could establish a modicum of trust—a rapport—with this deranged beast.

She had told him a long story about how she had struggled, growing up in a poor and dysfunctional family in Brantford, Ontario, and how she had left home at a young age, no longer able to tolerate her alcoholic father's verbal and physical abuse. Mentally scarred, she had disassociated herself from her family, striking out on her own, going to law school and finally, at the age of 37, hanging up her shingle as a corporate lawyer and only recently landing a lucrative contract with a large gambling organization looking to set up corporate structures that would allow them to pay much less in taxes.

Careful to keep the mention of her boyfriend, Nathan, out of the conversation for fear Thorvald would react jealously, she had also told him that's when her world—and *the* world—had come crashing down around her.

She had been surprised to see a tear welling in the big man's infected eye as she had told the story, and when he had gone on to tell her of the physical and psychological abuse he had suffered at the hands of his controlling father, he had put his hands to his face and begun sobbing, a flicker of humanity evident in his worn-out and contaminated features.

Too bad. I'm going to feel sorry for him when I kill him.

The conversation had eventually shifted to his interest in her. He had explained if she behaved herself that eventually they could develop a closer and more intimate relationship. In other words, he had planned on using her as his girl-toy, having his way with her when he wanted.

She had played along with the scenario, encouraging him to untie her. But that's when his mood had darkened and he had said, "If you think I'm stupid enough to give you trust just like that, you better think again. You have to earn my trust." With that statement he had smacked her in the face so hard she now bore a black and blue handprint on her cheek.

The stairs creaked and the big infected man lumbered down. He came into view holding a glass of water, chewing on a chunk of meat. Medium rare. Just how he liked it.

"I thought you might be thirsty," he said, setting the glass on a makeshift table beside the torn and dirty mattress. He wore a holstered pistol close to his armpit.

"I am," she squeaked.

"I'm going to untie you," he said, producing a large hunting knife. "If you try anything you'll get this and that," pointing to the knife and then the gun.

"Don't worry Thor," she said smiling. "Do you like that name?"

"I do ... the mighty Thor."

"That's you."

He bent down, cut the zip-ties binding her extremities. "There, now show me the shelter."

He sat back in a chair admiring her scantily clad body as she dressed. She pulled over a large green parka jacket, the last article of clothing, and felt for the handle. It was there, in an inside pocket, a small knife and some pepper spray. *He had been careless and he would pay. And I don't even think I'll feel sorry for him when I kill him. No. Not anymore.*

They climbed the stairs and reached the surface. Cadence frowned at the human leg still roasting on the open fire, pinched her nose, and felt the vomit rise up in her throat. She swallowed, trying to contain it, but it was no use. She coughed, bent her head and puked on the ground, hacking and spewing.

"You'll get used to it," Thorvald said, coughing and spitting up blood. He grimaced at the sight. "You'll have to eventually."

"Which way to the shelter?" he asked after she had stopped retching.

White-faced, she pointed south. "It's that way."

"Let's go then."

He grabbed her arm, pushing her in the lead. "I'll follow you, so you don't try anything."

Chapter Six

"Who's following who?" Nathan said.

"Didn't I just tell you?" Ed asked. It was a rhetorical question.

"Sorry, I was thinking of something." They had stopped for a short water break while walking through the network of tunnels, and as they were about to continue Nathan had become absorbed in thought and completely lost track of who was leading the show.

He had tossed and turned most of the night as various memories of his former life had started to resurface. But it was all bad shit and he knew there must be a good memory there somewhere. He just didn't know where or how to retrieve it yet.

It seemed to him he had been under a tremendous amount of stress just prior to a head injury of some sort. A fresh scar on the back of his thirty-seven-year-old head was the first indicator of the injury. But this morning Ed had been in a better mood and had filled him in on some other elements of his life. That he had worked as a newspaper reporter for The Guardian, a local paper. That he had fallen off the roof of his house while repairing it. That he had a "rather stunning" girlfriend, Cadence. *That's a good memory.* He had a very dim memory of Cadence's blue eyes, her sculptured body, quick smile, easy laugh, and flowing blonde hair.

But that's all there was. Nothing else. Just that, and the strange knowledge that somehow she was alive, and in danger of becoming very dead, very soon. The image in his mind's eye of her dying had haunted him for a good part of the night. He wasn't dreaming. He couldn't sleep, he was just imagining all the ways she could possibly die. He tried to push the thoughts from his mind and another negative and disturbing image had flooded forth.

It seemed he had owned a duplex somewhere in PEI and had had a bad experience trying to evict a delinquent tenant. The reprobate tenant had bounced a rent check and he hadn't noticed it for about two weeks. He had phoned the tenant a number of times, diplomatically requesting he make good on the rubber check. Two weeks went by and nothing. The tenant had been renting the unit for about six months and was always punctual with the rent so Nathan had begun to worry that Tyrone Clipper might actually be dead.

So he had located one of the man's references, his ex-wife Darlene, and got her on the phone. Explaining that he hadn't heard from Tyrone in over two weeks and there were some rental arrears, Nathan had asked the cooperative woman if she had heard from him.

Nathan remembered the conversation as if it were yesterday. "Oh, he's around alright," she had said. "I just talked to him yesterday to get him to sign the divorce papers. He doesn't return your calls? That doesn't surprise me. Tyrone has a history of avoidance. He thinks if he avoids his problems they'll go away. Why do you think I'm not with him anymore?"

Finally, Nathan had posted a 14-day eviction notice on the door of the duplex. A week went by and Tyrone still did not return any of his calls and would not acknowledge written 24-hour requests to show the suite to other prospective tenants. Nathan also noticed the exterior of the property littered with debris, oil stains on the sidewalk and Tyrone had decided the lawn, instead of the driveway, was a much better place to park his vehicle.

Nathan, who had been permanently psychologically scarred by a deranged tenant who had lasted fourteen months and done considerable damage on another rental property he had owned, finally became furious and the phone messages became less than polite.

In one of them, he had said, "Tyrone, it seems that you think if you avoid your problems they'll go away. While I'm here to tell you that's not the case. If you think you can mess with me you've picked the wrong fucking guy. I will be at the property at the expiration of the eviction notice with a sheriff, and you and your belongings will be kicked curbside. Govern yourself accordingly."

Tyrone, by his own admission a non-drinking Christian, did not respond to the call until a few days later. Nathan had received an email saying he had recorded the phone message, viewed it as a threat of violence and harassment, had video-taped Nathan banging on the door at one point and finished the email with a veiled threat; which was he would honor the eviction notice, but if Nathan tried to collect on any of the rental arrears, he would turn over his "evidence" to the RCMP and proceed with harassment charges.

Nathan had been pleasantly surprised to see the unit cleaned to an acceptable standard on the last day of the eviction notice, but had been troubled by the man's threats. And, one of the few things he could remember was an image of the man, about 240 pounds with a rotund stomach, wavy brown hair and a four-day growth. Nathan stood six foot one, and weighed in at a slender 175 pounds. Tyrone was easily six foot five. But, it seemed, the last phone call had scared the shit out of the cowardly delinquent and the only thing he could come up with to keep Nathan at bay was the threat of criminal charges.

In his entire lifetime, Nathan had never had a run-in with the law. That was the only thing that kept the arrears file labeled "bad debt" sitting on his desk. He remembered looking at it a few days after Tyrone had honored the eviction notice, wondering if he would turn it over to collections. He was hooked up with a fine collection agency in PEI that would automatically register every bad debt on the debtor's credit report. The only way the black mark could be removed was if the person paid the arrears to the bill collector. Otherwise, his credit would be ruined for life.

My pound of flesh.

What had kept Nathan from turning over the file to his bill collector was the veiled threat from Tyrone. Something in the email about this matter now being settled ... *I will accept no further communication from you ... I have preserved your phone calls threatening violence and videotaped your eviction process ... You are lying about the damages.*

The email had ended ... *Govern yourself accordingly,* Tyrone's last stab at vengeance.

Nathan had thought there was a principal involved here. Why was fear preventing him from taking revenge? Would the cops really do anything about a rather forceful message telling a delinquent tenant to honor an eviction notice? Would they do anything about an uncooperative tenant who had damaged the exterior of the property and, although Nathan had witness and photographic evidence, indicated in an email that Nathan was lying about the damages?

And what had Nathan possibly done on the video tape that could be so incriminating? He remembered only knocking on the door, Tyrone not answering, and posting and photographing an eviction notice.

The reality of his current situation cemented itself in his mind and he realized the whole nasty tenant business meant shit in comparison to the problems he had now. He didn't know what day it was, he lived in squalor, and there were repugnant enemies everywhere who wanted to occupy this cave, this shelter, and kill him for the privilege.

But there is something to it. Anger management issues here. And more. There's something to learn. Should I have forgotten the whole thing, moved on, or exacted the pound of flesh through the collector and let people know they can't fuck with me?

He didn't have the answer. And he didn't know why his memory was mostly recalling the bad shit in his life. *Would it ever remember the good stuff?*

Ed stopped abruptly and Nathan bumped into him. "Sorry," Nathan said.

"Watch where you're going."

"I can't see shit."

Ed bent down and kneeled in front of a large boulder, beaming the light around its perimeter and scratching the dirt away. "It's here."

"What?"

"It's another tunnel that I covered up. We need to go inside. Help me lift it."

"Why are we going in there?" *When am I going to stop asking stupid questions?*

"You killed a fucking Neanderthal, you idiot. They'll be coming for us. They'll break that steel door and kill us."

Nathan wasn't sure Ed's conclusions warranted a response so he bent down and they both strained, trying to slide the boulder over. It wouldn't budge and even combined the pair didn't have a lot of strength in their emaciated conditions.

Ed stood up scratching his head. A light bulb went on. "Wait here." He walked away, leaving Nathan alone in the dark with his thoughts. *Who's Cadence? My girlfriend. What kind of relationship did we have? Did I love her? I don't feel love. I don't remember love. What is love like anyway?*

A few minutes later, Ed returned with a large steel bar. Nathan smiled at him. He did not remember smiling in a long time. "Good thinking. Leverage."

"You're smarter than I thought," Ed said.

After a few minutes of grunting, they finally had the boulder propped precariously with the steel bar butted up against the wall of the cave.

"Get in," Ed said.

Nathan slid into the narrow opening. He guessed he had lost about thirty pounds since his incarceration in the shelter and he slipped through easily. Ed handed him the flashlight, slid into the hole, dropping to the ground, landing on his butt with a thud.

"Oww," Ed said.

"You okay?"

"Yeah. Let me see if I can get this thing to drop. Help me up."

"How?"

"Kneel down. I'll stand on your back."

"My back?"

"Do you have a better idea?"

"No."

"Then get down."

Nathan knelt down and Ed stepped up on his back, stood up and with a swift jerking motion pulled the steel bar away from the small opening.

The boulder crashed down, sealing the entrance and Ed jumped to the ground with the bar. He shone the flashlight at the ceiling for a few seconds and, satisfied that the opening was sufficiently hidden, turned to Nathan.

"Good job. Now let's hope they don't find it."

Chapter Seven

"Are you sure you can find it?" Thorvald asked, huddled under a man-made opening in a pile of debris.

The wind had intensified, the temperature colder than when they had set out four hours earlier. The sky was crimson red, an orange sunset beginning to crest the hostile landscape. Bits of debris and dust swirled in the wind.

"I'm sure," Cadence said, waving her arm. "It's about two hours that way."

It was now or never. She extracted the pepper spray, stood up and blasted Thorvald flush in the eyes.

Screaming, he instantly rushed blindly toward her.

She lunged at his throat with the knife but dumb luck was on his side. He grabbed her wrist and twisted her arm painfully.

She screamed, instinctively kicking him in the nuts. He doubled over in pain, moaning, slumping forward, releasing the steel grip on her wrist.

The shotgun. Go for the shotgun.

But Thorvald was already straightening his posture, his scab-marked face twisted with rage. He staggered forward, wiping his eyes.

Cadence blasted him with the pepper spray again, extracted the knife and plunged it deep into his chest.

What side is the heart on? Right or left? His left, my right. Shit, I stabbed him on my left, that's his lung.

He charged again and this time Cadence had to dive to avoid his reach. And, as he spun around, she rolled over, jumped up and grabbed the shotgun. As he stumbled forward coughing, screaming, yelling, "I'll kill you, you bitch," she leveled it at his head and pulled the trigger.

The blast sent him reeling backwards, bits of his skull rocketing in different directions. He crashed into a wall of debris and crumpled to the ground like an oversized ragdoll, lifeless.

Cadence stared at the dead body of Thorvald for a few minutes, wide-eyed and horrified by what she had just done. *Wake up girl, it was him or you.*

But that thought didn't stop the tears from coming. She dropped the gun on the ground, knelt down with her face in her hands and started crying softly. *What has this world come to, where we have to kill or be killed?*

"Is that your first one?"

The adrenaline pumping from her life and death struggle, Cadence initially thought the voice was inside her head. But then she heard the rumble of the engine, wiped her tears away and jerked upright.

A woman dressed in a black leather body suit, flowing black hair, sat in the driver's seat of a beat-up red Chevy pick-up truck, her eyes riveted on Cadence. She held a loaded cross bow and had it leveled at Cadence's head.

In her panic, Cadence had not even heard the vehicle approach. She would have to be much more careful if she wanted to survive in this dog-eat-dog environment.

She reached for the shotgun.

"Oh no you don't," Velvet Jones said, her focused eyes glancing at the crossbow, back to Cadence threateningly. She resembled a hardened Veronica Lodge from Archie comics who had somehow found herself stuck in a Mad Max movie.

"Is that your first one?" she asked again, glancing down at the bloodied corpse.

"Yeah."

"And it was hard."

"Yeah."

"Don't worry it'll get easier." She stepped out of the truck, crossbow drawn. "You're not going to fuck with me, are you?"

"No," Cadence said, pointing to the dead body. "He kidnapped me, threatened my life. I had no choice."

"Oh, we all have choices," Velvet said, approaching. "And you chose to live. That's a good thing." She glanced at the buckshot ridden, infected body lying on the ground, a red pool growing and encircling what remained of the head. "He would have died in a month from radiation poisoning anyway. I know the symptoms."

"You're not going to hurt me?"

"Hell, no. That is, not as long as you decide I'm a much better person to you alive than dead."

"I have no reason to hurt you. Will you help me?"

Velvet walked to within six inches of Cadence's face, stared unflinchingly into her eyes for what seemed like many minutes. It was only a few seconds. "Okay, I'll help you. But if you decide to betray my trust, turn on me, I won't hesitate to insert this little arrow here in your brain, right between your eyes. Is that crystal clear?"

Cadence shuddered. "Yeah."

They made introductions, shook hands. Something about Velvet was instantly fascinating to Cadence, overriding her fear. It was perhaps the sensitivity and intelligence deep in her penetrating green eyes, beyond the hardened surface that she found so attractive. Until now she had never even entertained the notion of sleeping with a woman, and she quickly dismissed the stirrings of sexual desire.

Velvet seemed to sense it and grinned mischievously, exposing perfectly aligned white teeth.

"Here," she said, producing a pair of leather work gloves. "Let's get whatever munitions he's got and get the fuck out of here."

Chapter Eight

"Get the fuck out of there," Karl demanded, looking into a hole at a fat man curled up in the fetal position, his hands held protectively to his face.

On route to the shelter, the Neanderthals had stopped at a pile of debris to forage for food and water. They were four, riding in the newly acquired 2005 Ford F350 Lariat—Karl, Russ, Arnie Jackman, and Bennie Frost.

Arnie and Bennie foraged through the debris while Karl and Russ examined their new captive, an ape of a man but as cowardly as a mouse being chased by a ravenous cat.

"What's your name?" Karl snapped. He hated cowards almost as much as he hated people who disrupted his concentration. He had a lot more respect for someone who would go down with a fight than he ever would for this chicken-shit motherfucker.

"Tyrone Clipper," the man said, finally removing his hands and squinting up at his captors.

"Tyrone Clipper," Karl said. "That sounds like a fucking baby's name, little boy. Are you a baby?"

"No," Tyrone whimpered.

"No, you're not a baby. Well then you're a big man with no stones, no balls, hombre, you get it?"

"Yeah," Tyrone said weakly.

They had pistols trained on him. "Get your fat ass out of the hole with your hands up," Karl said. "Tell me where your food supplies are, or you'll find yourself dead in a fucking hurry."

Tyrone stood, trembling with fear. "There's a sheet of plywood on top, over there."

"Arnie, lift up that wood over there, tell me what you find."

The burly, tattooed bald man walked over, kneeled down at the plywood and flipped it up in a swift motion. He rummaged around in the hole before finally smiling, pulling out some plastic bags with canned goods. "All kinds of shit in here boss."

Tyrone now stood topside, his arms raised high in the air, the corners of his lips turned down in a pout.

Karl and Russ regarded him while the other members loaded foodstuffs into the truck.

"Any more food supplies or is that it?" Karl asked.

"That's it," Tyrone said.

"You got any weapons on you?"

"No."

"You sure."

"No."

"What, you're not sure or you don't have any weapons? Which is it?"

"Just this," he said, producing a small hunting knife from his jeans pocket, handing it to Russ.

"Looks like this sissy's a fucking liar boss," Russ said, snatching the knife.

"You a fucking liar?" Karl asked. "Now don't lie to me."

"Yes," Tyrone said, his gaze shifting to the ground. "Sorry."

"You know," Karl said approaching, "there's only one thing I hate more than people who mess with my concentration and chicken-shits. And that's fucking liars." He smashed Tyrone in the side of the head with the butt end of his revolver and he staggered back, seeing stars. Karl took another step, smashed

Tyrone a second time in the temple and he fell hard to the ground and began blubbering and sobbing.

Karl fired a bullet into his kneecap and he screamed in pain, rolling and clutching the wound. "Please, take all you want, just don't kill me. There's another hole under that old tire over there."

Karl's face reddened with rage. "I thought you told me that was all the food supplies you had. You lied to me. What did I tell you about my feelings about liars?"

Before Tyrone could answer, Karl pointed the pistol at his crotch and fired two bullets.

Tyrone screamed again, grabbing his bloodied crotch, twisting on the ground in agony.

They took another five minutes to load all the supplies, while he writhed on the ground, his screams finally subsiding to a soft, steady wail.

"Put him out of his misery," Karl ordered as he hopped into the truck.

Russ approached the injured man, leveling the weapon. "Anything you want to say before you go to hell in a hand basket, motherfucker?"

Tyrone opened his mouth to speak, but before the words could be formed, Russ shot him twice, once in the mouth, once in the eye, and kicked him in the head—just because he could. His body twitched and went limp.

"You're a fucking waste of a human being," Russ said, kicking him a second time in the head and spitting in his face. "Cowardly piece of shit."

Russ hopped in the driver's seat, backed up over the body, slammed it into drive and floored it. The tires spun dirt and gravel, connected with Tyrone and spit chunks of his flesh and clothing out the ass-end as they found traction, the Neanderthals guffawing with laughter as they headed toward the shelter.

Chapter Nine

"This looks like a well-equipped shelter," Nathan observed.

They had slid down a narrow tunnel, about as long and roughly the same angle as a slide in a kid's playground, and landed in a large, roughly-hewn room consisting of large boulders and rock walls. Three cave corridors led in different directions. Ed had walked over to a metal storage shed, opened it and pulled out a number of supplies, including some packaged food, cans, bottled water, and protein bars.

There were garbage cans strategically placed at all corners of the room, and a large pile of wood off to one side, close to one of the cave corridors. There was no debris like the last bunker. This place was a planned refuge, although it was damp, dark and rocky.

"I put a little thought into it," Ed said, handing Nathan an LED flashlight and a protein bar.

"Why didn't we stay here before?"

"This is phase two of our survival. I wanted to use up the supplies in the other unit first, make it appear to be the only good refuge in the cave system. So when we're invaded, which will be soon, they'll think we fled. They won't have any evidence or reason to believe otherwise."

"What else do you have in here?"

"Well, I was just stocking it when the bomb went off and I didn't get a chance to finish. But, those two doors go to separate bedrooms, the other one there goes to the ocean."

"Any weapons?"

"Yeah."

He walked over to another wooden box, cranked open the wooden lid with a nearby crowbar, revealing rifles, handguns, shotguns, and AK-47s. An arsenal.

Nathan peered inside. "We could've used these for the Neanderthal."

"I know," Ed said, staring at his hands. "Listen I haven't been thinking all that clearly lately. Neither have you, for that matter. You can't remember anything. But my wife was in New Brunswick when the bomb, or bombs, hit and I'm sure she's dead. That shit's hard to take."

Nathan stood silent for a long while, feeling a wave of compassion. Up until now he had viewed Ed as a gruff man with a very short fuse. But it wasn't that simple. It never was. He had been grieving and they had been close to starving for the last three months because Ed was sick with heartbreak. For Nathan it was easier. Other than a faint recollection of Cadence, he didn't remember much else, including this mysterious man standing beside him, crunching on a protein bar.

And, Nathan had made a point not to ask Ed about *his* family, about *his* relationship with Cadence. He wasn't sure he was psychologically ready for too much information right now. He only knew he was under a hell of a lot of stress prior to his amnesia-producing fall. He knew some of the reasons why, but not all of them. They would probably come to him tonight, when he wandered off to his new bedroom and tried to catch some shut eye.

I hope Tyrone Clipper got blown to pieces in the blast, the little fuck.

Ed walked over to the pile of wood, started breaking off bits of kindling. Soon, he had a small fire blazing and Nathan sat next to him on a white plastic chair. He had noticed this cave, much lower in elevation, wasn't nearly as cold as the other one.

The smoke from the flame was sucked into the small passageway that led to the ocean. They sat silently looking at the dancing flames, alone with their thoughts. A few minutes passed.

"Want some tea?" Ed asked, rising and fishing through a wooden box.

"Sure."

Ed pulled out a new green kettle, filled it with bottled water and hung it over the flames. He looked at the fire somberly and said nothing.

Nathan had a lot of fears about this new world, about which he knew practically nothing. He felt like a character from William Golding's *Lord of the Flies*, in which a group of young boys get stranded on a remote island and it doesn't take long before many of them resort to violence, savagery, and cold-blooded murder. Their dark instincts go beyond sheer survival, depicting humans as a race capable of gratuitous and unprovoked acts of unfathomable evil after the disintegration of law and order.

Is that what's happening here? Nathan wondered. *The meltdown of mankind as a rational being, which would perhaps give way to a new order, the evolution of a new kind of human being. Or would another species take over, would man's existence become extinct, like the dinosaur?* He didn't know and he pushed the thought from his mind as the kettle started to whistle.

Ed poured the tea, set the teapot down, and took a seat.

They sipped for a few minutes in silence.

"Do we have any plan other than to stay here until our food runs out?" Nathan finally asked.

Ed removed his hypnotic gaze from the fire. "I heard after the blast that Newfoundland was also spared a direct hit. My wife saw something on CNN and called to warn me. The line went dead halfway through her info, but she said getting there would be my only chance of survival."

Nathan had no idea what Newfoundland was but didn't want to risk pissing Ed off any more than he had to. "Do you know if this information is true?"

"No. All electronic communication is down. I have no idea how many survivors are out there, how many countries have been affected, if the war is even over. But I don't have any better ideas. Do you?"

Nathan shook his head, wanting to hear more. "How do we get to Newfoundland?"

"We build a boat and sail there."

"How do we do that?"

"With the material outside. We slowly work at it. Once we have it constructed, we leave."

"You plan on taking anyone else, besides us."

"You trust anyone else?"

Nathan didn't even know if he could trust Ed. "I don't know."

"To trust is to expose yourself unnecessarily to death," Ed said. "And I'm not prepared to do that."

"What about radiation?" Nathan said. "Is it gone, or are we still in danger of being exposed, dying from exposure?"

"I don't know anything about radiation exposure. All I know is it's been over three months since the bomb dropped and there's been a hell of a lot of nasty, windy weather in between. My hope is that the levels are low enough so we won't die, but I have no idea really. I did notice some stomach nausea while we were outside the other day, but it passed. You?"

"I felt a little sick too, but it seemed to pass."

"Keep these on when you're outside," pointing to some yellow rubber gloves protruding from the wooden box. "And get a new pair every time."

There was a pause and Nathan finally asked, "Was I a nice person? Am I a nice person?"

Ed poked at the fire with a metal poker, repositioning the kettle to boil position. "You want some more tea?"

"Sure."

Another pause. "Overall you're alright, I guess. You definitely have some asshole tendencies, but who doesn't? Do you like every single thing about every single friend? No, you don't. You have to figure out if the good outweighs the bad. Decide what you can tolerate, what you can't. It's not a perfect world, you know."

"Especially not now," Nathan agreed. He could remember nothing about Ed, not even his face was familiar to him; although snippets of his own life, the bad stuff, was starting to come back. He was about to ask him when his ears picked up a faint scraping sound, seemingly coming from the cave opening that led to the ocean. "Did you hear that?"

Ed jumped to his feet, walked to the wooden box and extracted two AK-47 assault rifles, one of the most popular and practical killing machines on Earth. He loaded magazines into both weapons, removed the safeties, and handed one to Nathan.

He gave him a quick whispered instruction on how to handle the weapon. They backed up from the opening and fell silent, guns drawn.

But for the odd popping and crackling of the fire, they heard nothing. Ed shone the small flashlight into the abyss, but the blackness swallowed the light and the black hole was the only thing visible. There was too much depth and blackness for the small flashlight to make any kind of a noticeable difference.

Nathan wanted more than anything to be out of this nightmare, home safely in bed somewhere far removed from this struggling existence. He would do almost anything for a hot shower, a cold beer, and a cigarette. *Cigarette? Oh, that's right I smoke. Or used to. There, I remembered something else.*

He heard a scurrying sound in the corner of the cave and pointed his beam, stepping backward as he did and almost tripping on a rock. He could feel cold goose bumps crawling up his arms and back. The beam, like a yellow stain, danced around the wall, finally fixing on a pair of small yellow eyes. A rat. The rat stared at him, unmoving, unwavering. Then, a different sound from the hole.

A scraping sound, dull and echoing faintly through the chamber at first but gradually getting louder.

This unwelcome intrusion meant their shelter was no longer secure, if it ever had been. Somehow, somewhere further down the line, maybe at the ocean level, there was an access point. One that would have to be sealed off until they could think their way out of this dark and dungeon-like existence. Was there even a way out? Or was it simply their time to die?

"Who's there?" Ed said. "And what do you want?"

Just the scraping, coming closer, like the sound of a fingernail on a chalkboard.

"Who goes there?" Ed said. "Announce yourself and your motives or we'll shoot to kill!"

Nathan shone the flashlight beam into the hole again and thought he saw something other than the obscurity of darkness. A hand. A waving hand.

Suddenly a hoarse, pain-filled voice of a man echoed up through the tunnel. "Shoot if you want, I'm dead anyway."

"Hold your fire," Ed ordered.

Nathan supposed he had a new boss. He raised his gun in the air, continuing to focus on the image, that was now much more than a waving hand. A middle-aged man limped out of the darkness dragging his left leg which dangled at an unnatural angle behind him. He had broken it badly and his blue jeans were torn and tattered and stained red from the hip down. They could have passed for red pants, but the right leg was blue. His white t-shirt was torn and stained dark red. His forearms bore large gashes, evidently the result of a struggle for his life.

He had long grey, disheveled hair that was matted to one side of his head by more blood, probably the result of blunt force trauma.

As he got closer they saw lines creasing his face, his cheeks blistering and oozing with puss and blood. He stopped about three feet in front of them and vomited, a red and yellow sticky mixture that spewed forth with such force it bounced of the rock bed below, some of it splattering back up to his face.

I don't have the stomach for this, Nathan thought.

"Are you armed?" Ed asked after the hacking and puking subsided.

"Not anymore," the man said, spitting, glancing at the fire.

Nathan dropped his machine gun, ran to him, putting an arm over his shoulder, guiding him to a white plastic chair by the fire. He poured some water into a glass and offered it to the man. The man took it, draining it instantly and coughed some more. "You're losing a lot of blood," Nathan said, as the white chair quickly became covered with the man's blood. The man grunted and held the tin cup out for more water. Nathan refilled it and he drained it in one long gulp.

Nathan rummaged through one of the supply boxes, tore some strips of cloth off an old t-shirt, wrapped the pieces around the man's leg and arms, trying to stem the blood flow, prolong his life a little longer; although, he knew, regardless of his efforts, this man didn't have long to live. He also bandaged the head wound with a torn cloth.

Then he grabbed an old blanket, threw it around the man's slender frame, and Ed and Nathan joined him at the fire. When the man's labored breathing had slowed to something resembling normal, Ed finally said, "I'm Ed, this is Nathan. And you are?"

"I'm Aiden James. And whatever you do, don't go outside. It's gotten ugly." He shivered in spite of the thick wool comforter draped over him.

Ed fixed three hot mugs of tea and distributed them while Aiden explained what happened. He had surfaced from a root cellar on his property he had been surviving in. It was the third time he had surfaced to gather canned goods, packaged food from what was left of his house. That's when he was attacked by four men in a black pick-up truck. They had smashed him in the head a few times with a bat, crushed his leg by running over it with a truck, slashed his arms during the initial struggle and left him for dead after stealing what food and valuables they could find. They probably would have put a few bullets in his head had it not been for a radiation-exposed pig he kept on his farm that had attacked one of the men, clamping into one of his legs and tearing away large chunks of flesh.

As well, the weather had taken a nasty turn for the worse and a severe windstorm had blown in, faint echoes of its impending force only now becoming audible from the tunnel to the ocean.

Aiden had limped down to his dock, boarded his motorized fishing boat and started chugging around the island until he discovered a cave along one of the inlets. He tied the boat off after guiding it down the narrow passageway, finally limping his way up to Ed's bomb shelter. As he told the story, he stopped many times to cough and spit blood.

"There's nothing left of our humanity," he said, swallowing the last drop of tea in his mug.

Nathan stood, refilled it and sat down. "You have a boat?"

"Yeah, it's anchored near your cave."

"Does it still run? Does it have fuel?"

"It runs great," Aiden said. "I used to be a lobster fisherman and *Delilah Blue* is my baby. Only problem, I don't have much diesel fuel. There's enough to get you maybe twenty miles out to sea, then you're at the mercy of Mother Nature."

He produced a key from his pocket and tossed it on the ground. "It's yours. I don't have long with the living. I can see the way you guys are looking at me. I might be almost dead but I'm not stupid. Besides, I don't think I waited long enough when I first left my shelter. I think the first trip out gave me a fatal dose of radiation, my days were numbered after that." He coughed and spit blood in the fire, his expression becoming resigned, his eyes glazing over; the hopeless expression of a man coming to terms with his mortality.

"Did you see any other people out there?" Nathan asked.

"No, just the scumbags who attacked me."

"They're the Neanderthals," Ed said. "We killed one of them."

"Good for you," Aiden said. "I hope they rot in hell."

"Looks like they are," Nathan said, instantly regretting his words.

"One more thing," Aiden said, his voice barely a whisper now. "Something very strange is happening to the animals. My pig, Arnold, was as docile as a pussy cat before the radiation exposure. Now, he's become like a rabid dog, sick with radiation and an agenda to kill humans. You should have seen the ferocity with which he attacked that scumbag."

Nathan tried to force the thought from his mind but couldn't. *An evolutionary change. Animals getting even at mankind for our stupidity. The pecking order reversed.*

"That's not the only thing," Aiden said, "I was attacked by a fox on my way to the boat, had to beat him off with a chunk of metal. And I had seagulls attacking me when I boarded *Delilah Blue.* One of them tore a chunk of skin off my shoulder." He lifted the blanket, pulled back his bloodied t-shirt, exposing a V-shaped cut on his shoulder, the blood just beginning to clot.

"Would you like more tea?" Ed asked.

Aiden nodded. His face had become paler.

Ed repositioned the kettle and after a few minutes refilled the mugs. Aiden's head had dropped to one side and his eyes closed.

"Aiden," Ed said, handing him a mug. His eyes slowly opened and he received the hot drink.

Ed retrieved a few more logs and stoked the fire. He picked at it with a metal poker while Nathan watched Aiden slowly sip his tea.

"What're you guys planning to do?" Aiden asked.

"We were thinking of going to Newfoundland, The Rock. Heard anything about it? I heard it was out of the blast zone, with any luck the radiation exposure zone as well," Ed said.

"I heard that too," Aiden said. "And that was my plan." He was silent for a moment and then fished out a gold necklace with a small locket and a crumpled envelope and set the items on his lap.

"Could you guys do me a favor?" He looked at Nathan.

"Sure," Nathan said. "Anything."

"I've been estranged from my daughter, Melissa, for a very long time. Her mother ran out on me before I even knew of her existence. When she was six, I find out I have a daughter. I start visiting, sending money. Then, on one visit, after I arrive home her mother accuses me of being a bad role model, says she never wants me to ever contact Melissa again. She's fourteen now. Says I smoke pot around her, encouraged her to date boys at a very young age, and taught her to disrespect her mother."

"Is any of that true?" Nathan asked.

"No," Aiden said, using what little strength he had left to raise his voice. "Lenora is a control freak, wants to control our little girl. I would never think of exposing my daughter to any of that. I want the best for her. I miss her. I love her. If you make it to The Rock, could you tell her that?"

Nathan and Ed watched intently, nodding.

Aiden picked up the necklace and letter, extending them. "And please, give her this locket, this le ..." Aiden took a last gasp, closed his eyes, and died. His hand dropped to his lap, the fingers curled tightly around the items. The metal mug dropped to the ground, clanging and clattering hollowly.

Nathan stood up, slowly pried his fingers apart and removed the items. He straightened the envelope, set it down on a supply box and stared at the locket. He fought to control the lump growing in his throat.

"Aren't you going to open it?" Ed said.

The gold locket was about half the size of the old style pocket watches. Nathan unclasped it, opened it up. There was a picture of Aiden in much brighter days, smiling, his thick grey hair neatly cropped in a brush cut, his blue eyes looking intently at the photographer. He was dressed in a black suit, white shirt, and dark green tie.

Inside the locket, were words etched into the gold: *Dearest Melissa, I will always love you. Your dad, Aiden.*

Nathan brushed away a tear, hoping Ed hadn't noticed.

"Well, read it to me," Ed said.

Nathan repeated it and sat down somberly. *Another day in paradise.*

Chapter Ten

"This isn't another day in paradise," Velvet said sternly. "Here you have to work for your food, for your survival."

Cadence lay on a cot in a mechanic pit below the floor of an old barn that had been converted to a shop. Velvet's pick-up truck was directly above them. Cadence's entire body ached and her head throbbed with a dull pain. After Velvet had rescued her, they had driven to the hideout, bordered by a large debris pile—the efforts of Velvet to create a sort of security perimeter.

Cadence thought she had been there for at least two nights, but wasn't sure. No clocks functioned and they did not enjoy the benefit of cell phones or Internet. Time seemed to have no relevance unless you gave it relevance.

They had survived on canned food: Corn, beans, bottled water and some multivitamins. Velvet wouldn't risk killing any of the rabbits they had noticed, claiming they were probably contaminated with radiation. She wasn't sure but wasn't prepared to take the chance.

The small pit had two LED flashlights hung in corners providing sparse light. There was an old couch, an armchair, coffee table, two cots, a kitchen table, and two chairs in a corner, boxes of various supplies piled high beside it. A large aluminum garbage can also stood beside the table, overflowing with refuse. Bits of garbage were also strewn around the can, but at least Velvet kept a reasonably clean household. At least she tried to contain the garbage in one area of the small dwelling so they wouldn't be tripping over things.

Velvet worked a pick-axe and shovel in another corner of the room, digging an emergency tunnel to provide another layer of protection from the predators. Cadence had dutifully performed shifts of a few hours—she didn't know, couldn't measure how many hours—for the last few nights and they were making some progress. They were down about twenty feet and had a hole with a four-foot circumference. There was a wheelbarrow inside the hole and, after filling it, Velvet dumped the contents into a damaged section of the pit, reinforcing one part of her abode while expanding another. Killing two birds with one stone.

Cadence thought about requesting a little nap before her shift started but she didn't think Velvet would take kindly to it. She was a take-charge woman who wanted her guests to follow her instructions. It was her house, her rules, after all.

Soaked in sweat, her black t-shirt beginning to cling tightly, Velvet dumped a load of dirt into the damaged section of the former mechanic pit. She had already told Cadence once to begin her shift. She wasn't going to say it again. She parked the empty wheelbarrow alongside Cadence, breathing heavily. Her green eyes regarded her guest insistently. "Well?"

Cadence slowly rose. "Okay. I know it's my turn."

Velvet removed her hardhat, jury-rigged with a flashlight, and placed it on Cadence's head, sliding her hand softly across her cheek and smiling. It seemed her moods would swing from black to white in an instant. She slumped on the armchair and Cadence picked up the wheelbarrow and went into the tunnel, her sore muscles, unaccustomed to hard labor, screaming a painful but unheard litany of objections.

She mechanically began shoveling loose dirt and gravel into the wheelbarrow and became absorbed in her thoughts. She had a rough idea where Ed's shelter was but could not pinpoint it exactly. Did it matter since Velvet was reluctant to venture too far from the protection of her fortress? She had mentioned the idea to her the other day over a dinner of canned pork, beans, and corn, but Velvet had steadfastly refused, claiming she wanted to make her stand right where she was, in spite of the danger from the Neanderthals. This was her home and she would die here.

But, if they were attacked, and really it wasn't a question of if, it was a question of when, wouldn't she see the logic in trying to get to Ed's shelter, an old abandoned mineshaft consisting of a network of tunnels that offered many more opportunities for defense and safety than where they were now?

Cadence reviewed her options. She didn't want to risk going alone, especially since she had heard horrible stories of the mutant animal attacks and the ruthless robbing and killing by the Neanderthals. No. She wanted an ally, and a resilient, resourceful one like Velvet.

But, what if she arrived only to discover the shelter was already overrun by the Neanderthals? She was sure they had it in their sights. Hell, they were probably on their way over their right now for all she knew.

And what about Nathan? She missed him terribly, but would he even remember her, if he was even still alive? And, if he didn't remember, they would have to start all over again, building trust and new memories. But did he even have the capacity to remember anymore? After the accident his short and long-term memory had become severely impaired. She had to tell him what they had done the previous day and he often looked at her blankly, vacant of the endearing, affectionate looks of the past.

But she wasn't even sure if she wanted a relationship anymore. The all-consuming need for food and survival seemed to overcome all others, even love. It took a backseat, she supposed, to the very real struggle for self-preservation.

But you can't stay here anyway. You'll die here. You still have to see the shelter, find out if he's alive. And you'll be safer there, even if you have to kill every one of those fucking Neanderthals and shore up the defenses.

The small flashlight taped to her hardhat went out but at the same time a light illuminated in her head. *Make a pass at Velvet. Win her favor with sexual advances, get her to take you to the shelter.*

It was obvious the woman liked her. Why not take advantage of the physical attributes she had the good fortune to be born with?

She ignored her screaming muscles, resolutely shoveled the dirt in the wheelbarrow, taking load after load after load, at one point even winking at Velvet, who by this time was engrossed in a novel, stretched out on the couch, occasionally glancing at her as she passed. Cadence even went so far as to remove her bra from inside her tight white t-shirt and continued working, her nipples, desirably curvaceous breasts, protruding visibly from the now sweat-soaked t-shirt.

On one return trip she noticed Velvet had adjusted her position, pointing her head at an angle allowing an unobstructed view of Cadence entering and leaving the tunnel.

Velvet no longer had to crane her neck to admire the object of her desire.

Finally, she finished and plunked down beside Velvet on the beaten couch. Velvet had by that time closed her novel, the critically acclaimed post-apocalyptic thriller, *Metro 2033*, by Dmitry Glukhovsky, and moved to one side of the couch, allowing ample room for Cadence to sit down.

"You made good progress," Velvet said.

"Thanks." And, staring into this mysterious woman's eyes she saw for the first time something she had never noticed before. Below the tough exterior, Cadence could see sadness deep in those eyes and wondered how many friends and loved ones the woman had lost. She wondered what her story was, knowing that everyone had a story, some with much more pain and suffering than others. She was curious to hear Velvet's story but perhaps not right now. Right now she had a mission to fulfill and she hoped to manipulate this sexy woman beside her into helping her fulfill that mission. "Do you have any wine?"

"As a matter of fact I do," Velvet said, walking to a cardboard box beside the table, pulling out an unlabeled bottle of red wine, a couple of coffee mugs and a corkscrew. She returned, sat down, opened the wine and filled the two cups.

"Cheers," Cadence said. "To our new alliance."

They clinked cups and drank. It was the first bit of alcohol Cadence had had in months and she enjoyed its tangy flavor, twirling the liquid in her mouth, savoring it a few seconds before swallowing it.

It didn't take long for the liquid panty-remover to do its job.

A few minutes later they were wrapped in an embrace, Cadence kissing Velvet passionately long and full on the lips, exploring her erogenous zones. In a world so full of pain and suffering, she delighted in Velvet's soft caress, her musky smell, lean athletic body, perky breasts, flowing black hair. She emptied her mind of its problems and took intense pleasure in the moment, the escape, the blissful sensations tingling through her entire body, her entire being. *Never mind tomorrow. I have this right now.*

Chapter Eleven

"We have to get rid of this right now," Ed said, pointing at the corpse of Aiden Jones.

Nathan rummaged through the arsenal, methodically laying each weapon on the ground and examining it. They had two rifles, two Colt 45 pistols, two AK-47 assault rifles, knives, some ammunition, and a crossbow. Hell, they even had a 12-gauge double-barrel sawed-off shotgun.

Ed had just finished giving him another crash course on handling the weaponry, lit a fire, and he sat around it now, drinking his tea, after breakfasting on protein bars and water.

Last night, curled up in layers of blankets, a small LED flashlight in hand, Nathan had thought he heard faint footsteps above him and even fainter voices. *They're here*, he had thought, shivering with fear. *How long before they find us and kill us?*

His memory was increasing marginally. He now seemed to remember a few days in the past. But, how many he wasn't sure, the whole concept of time seemingly obliterated along with the rest of the planet. He had tried hard to remember his past. But, for the most part, the only images that surfaced were scenes of yelling at people over uncollected debts. He couldn't remember the circumstances, other than the delinquent tenant memory, but the underlying emotion had surfaced. And it was an emotion largely unfamiliar to him until now—rage. He remembered wanting to kill those who owed him money, those who thought they could fuck with him.

I'm nice, they step all over me. I'm nasty, they're terrified of me. In better times, Nathan might not have favored this sentiment, but now he lived under a whole new set of rules, rules where people killed for food and just for the sheer joy of it. These new rules needed a brand new temperament, a brand new savagery if one wanted to survive. So he took some comfort in the raw edge he had discovered about himself. He didn't know if it had always been there, lurking below the surface, waiting patiently for the right opportunity to spew forth with a violent fury, or it was something entirely new. He simply couldn't remember. But he realized now he was capable of unfathomable acts of violence.

He had started to wonder if he would descend into complete madness and be unable to cope with his newfound primitive existence. All the violent thoughts had been piling up in his mind, threatening to come bursting forth as he lay on the old mattress. He searched for something positive and couldn't find it. Absently putting his hand in his pocket, he felt the crunchy paper of the letter, the gold locket. He had sat up in bed, shone the flashlight on the blood-smeared envelope, read the locket over and over again, until he had noticed the envelope had not been sealed properly. Unable to control the violent thoughts lashing around in his mind, he had gently opened the letter without tearing it.

Inside was a picture of a small blonde-haired girl, no older than ten, wrapped in an embrace with her beaming father, innocently and gleefully smiling at the photographer, lush green trees and a golden sun in the background. He flipped it over. Hand-written in blue ink it said: *To Melissa with lots of love. Your dad, Aiden.*

Unable to contain his curiosity, grasping at something, anything, to pull him out of the black abyss of dismal thought and emotion, he had opened the letter and read it.

To my daughter, Melissa.

I'm so sorry that for the last few years I have had so little contact with you. I hate to say anything negative about your mother as she has raised you well and has done her very best for you. And one thing I don't want you to do after you read this is to disrespect her. Please respect and obey her.

I have always tried to be a very good role model for you and I know at times I have slipped in this area. But I always wanted the best for you and always tried to raise you in a positive way; with respect for your elders, the proper amount of discipline, and love and caring.

I never told you this before as I thought you were too young. But, when your mother was pregnant with you she ran out on me and I didn't even know she was pregnant. I'm not saying she didn't have a right to run away. I was drinking a lot back then, had some serious money problems, was suffering from severe depression, and I was starting to act violently. Don't misunderstand me please. I never laid a hand on your mother and I didn't act out my violent impulses other than to punch walls, kick doors, and do a lot of swearing.

So, I wasn't a good candidate for a husband or a father and I don't blame your mother for leaving. But I didn't even know about your existence until you were six, in case you were wondering why I wasn't part of your life when you were younger. I didn't want to tell you this before, but I think something is terribly wrong with our world and I don't know how much time we have.

By the time your mother had contacted me, I was a different person. No longer drinking, my financial mess all cleaned up, and I settled on this farm where I live now. I learned from my mistakes, Melissa. I became a better person. I changed. And once I learned about you, it gave me another reason to change.

That's why every year, except for the last three, I have travelled to Boston to visit you. Three years ago, your mother decided I was a bad role model and cut off communication. This has been very hard on me, but I didn't know what to do. I did not want to put you in the middle of our disagreement. But now we're running out of time.

And I didn't do the things she said.

I hope when you get older you will understand the situation better, and one day I hope you can come and live with me on the farm, even if it's just for a year or two. I think I have a lot to offer you and would love the chance to be a positive influence and role model in your life.

I will close my dear. Remember you will always occupy a very special place in my heart. You are everything that's good in me and I know you will go on to make something useful with your life. You have all the potential in the world. You just have to realize it.

I hope to see you soon. Love, your dad Aiden. Lots of hugs.

Reading it had calmed Nathan and he had carefully folded it, returned the picture and resealed the envelope, satisfied that no one would be able to tell it had been opened. *The letter saved me. So far.*

"Did you hear me?" Ed snapped.

Nathan had an uncanny ability to concentrate on multiple things simultaneously. He knew this was rare as usually women were considered to be the best multi-taskers. It was not a trait typical of the male species. He had been thinking about the letter, churning over Ed's instructions on the weaponry, had heard and processed the comment about the corpse, had even decided the best place for it. They certainly couldn't live with it decaying in their presence.

"Why don't we dump it in the ocean," Nathan said, picking up his tea and joining Ed at the fire.

A few minutes later, two dark silhouettes holding flashlights, AK-47s strapped around their shoulders, pulled a heavy corpse down a dark tunnel toward the ocean. Aiden's head clunked on the odd rock as it was dragged along the ground. Ed and Nathan were now halfway to the water, drenched in sweat from the hard labor, their undernourished physical condition rendering the task formidable.

Breathing heavily, they finally arrived at a large dark cave, filled with sea water and dead fish. It was long and winding and offered no glimpse of where it might lead to the ocean. A few feet away, *Delilah Blue* was tied to a rock, the 36-foot fishing vessel gently rolling in the small waves.

"Is there anything you want to say?" Nathan said as they rolled the cadaver next to the water.

"About what?"

"About him."

"What am I going to say? I never knew him."

Nathan wasn't a religious man but he had to say something. He just couldn't roll him into a watery grave and say nothing. "In the short time I knew Aiden, I think he had a good heart. And I hope that he moves on to a better place, and finds peace in his heart and in his soul."

They kneeled down, rolling the dead body into the water with a splash. As Nathan stood up, he heard a screeching sound and turned his head. The sound disappeared and he looked at Ed, wide-eyed with fear. "Did you hear that?"

"Hear what?"

"Like screeching or chirping ... something."

"All I heard was the splash of a dead body."

"I thought I he ..."

The dark cave became loud with a high-pitched chirping sound and the fluttering of wings. Nathan felt it before he knew what it was. Small stinging sensations, first on his head, then arms and legs. Instantly, he pointed the flashlight. Birds.

Seagulls, and a flock so thick he could feel the wind from their wings.

"Fuck sakes," Ed said, waving the machine gun, spraying the air with bullets.

Nathan was slower to react. As he reached for his weapon, he tripped on the ground, felt the stinging bites on his back, neck and head. He rolled, grabbed the weapon, aimed it up into the black and grey mass and fired—rat-a-tat-tat, rat-a-tat-tat, rat-a-tat-tat.

An injured seagull dropped on in his head, squawking and rolling off. Nathan heard plunks and splashes as others died and dropped to the ground, into the water.

To his left, he could see Ed, brandishing the weapon with one hand, the flashlight in the other, spraying bullets, yelling, "Come here you motherfuckers and meet your maker. Come on, come on ..."

"Let's get the fuck out of here," Nathan said, wiping his blood-smeared face. Ed appeared in a trance, yelling, firing, fixated on killing and nothing else. Nathan grabbed his arm. "Let's go."

Ed's glazed eyes focused, staring at Nathan. He was smiling. "Let's kill them all."

Pulling at Ed, "We can't—there's too many."

He backed up, firing, tugging on Ed's sleeve with his free hand until they reached the small opening that wound its way up to their home. They crouched in the entrance, pointing the machine guns out, both simultaneously killing mutant birds. Finally the screeching faded into the distance and, but for one or two that had gone astray and still flew listlessly around, the cave emptied.

"Fuck, this is right out of an Alfred Hitchcock movie," Nathan said, finding no humor in the statement, examining his arms with the flashlight, seeing surgical V-shaped incisions oozing blood.

Ed stared blankly ahead, panting, his machine gun cocked, poised for another attack. But the birds did not return and the cave grew quiet, except for the fearful and labored breathing of its inhabitants. Nathan could hear his rapid heartbeat thumping and breathed deeply to calm himself.

Ed's glazed expression focused on the blackness ahead.

"Let's go," Nathan said, pulling at his sleeve. "They might come back."

It snapped Ed from his trance and he stared into Nathan's eyes blankly. They walked up the winding tunnel and, upon arriving in their dimly lit domain, sealed the entrance to the ocean with a large sheet of plywood and a few boulders to secure it into place.

Ed was stoking the fire when they abruptly heard it. Faint voices and footsteps above them. Had the Neanderthals discovered their hideout?

Chapter Twelve

"There it is—that's their hideout," Cadence said, pointing to an opening that once had a metal door sealing it. Someone had riddled the door with bullets, entered and closed it haphazardly behind them. It was heavily damaged by gunfire, dangling precariously on one hinge.

"It looks like someone got here before us," Velvet said, after skidding to a stop in her vehicle, rolling down the window and pointing the crossbow at the entrance. Just in case.

Cadence frowned. "Maybe the Neanderthals."

"I wouldn't doubt it. But I don't see a vehicle."

"Maybe they don't have a vehicle. Or maybe it's somewhere else, waiting."

They sat in silence for moment, both wondering what to do.

After their intense lovemaking session last night, Cadence had convinced Velvet to try and locate the shelter, telling her it would offer much more protection than what she was calling home. Velvet had protested initially but finally acquiesced.

After driving through the desolate wasteland for a few hours, Cadence was able to pinpoint the location. She knew it was close to the ocean and the island was small, so it was only a matter of time before she recognized the rock outcrop marking the shelter.

She had felt a little guilty for manipulating Velvet and finally confided in her she actually had a boyfriend, Nathan, whom she hoped was alive. In case they did discover him alive, she didn't want to alienate Velvet, whom she viewed as a potentially good ally.

At the news Velvet had stared at her knowingly and said: "Listen sister, I might have been born in a day, but it certainly wasn't fucking yesterday. I didn't attach anything to our little session other than a few hours of casual sex. It was what it was and it was great. If it happens again, great. If it doesn't, well who fucking cares."

There was an uncomfortable silence in the vehicle after that until Cadence had recognized the bomb shelter and they resumed conversation again.

Cadence slung a rifle over her shoulder, checked her holster ensuring the pistol was in place and ran her fingers along the two hunting knives she had sheathed around her waist. Satisfied she was properly armed, she opened the door and climbed out of the vehicle.

"Where you going, sister?" Velvet asked.

"Let's go," Cadence said.

"I'm not going in there. This is where we part company."

Maybe Cadence had admitted her attachment to Nathan too soon? "Please, I need your help!"

"I've given you my help. You wanted to get to the shelter. You're here. You're on your own now."

"I thought we were friends, allies?"

Velvet didn't answer the question. "I'm not going in there. It's too risky. You have five seconds to make up your mind. Come with me, or go in there, probably to your death." Velvet held out five fingers and counted.

Cadence stared blankly at her only protector.

"... three, two, one. Have a nice life," she said, slamming the vehicle into drive and pulling away quickly.

"Wait, wait," Cadence pleaded, watching the image of the truck become smaller as it rolled along the crimson landscape. She shuddered as she saw a large flock of shrieking seagulls suddenly change direction overhead and begin a descent aiming their attack at the disappearing vehicle. Finally, the red truck, the trailing flock of screeching birds, disappeared. She wiped a tear from her eye. "You sure fucked that up," she said, wondering what terrible fate Velvet would meet.

Wiping another tear away, she turned, pulled open the iron door and entered the cave entrance. She moved along in darkness, the small flashlight barely illuminated passage. *What am I doing? I should have stayed with Velvet.*

She came to a fork in the system of tunnels, stopped and jumped just as a rat squeaked and scurried away. She put her hand over her mouth to prevent a scream, holding it there a few seconds until the urge subsided. She stood silent, listening, hearing only the steady thud of her pounding heartbeat. She listened again. *What's that? Voices.*

She entered the hole where the sounds faintly echoed. After five minutes of walking, she noticed a small, dancing orange light just ahead and the conversations became louder, more animated. *Nathan? It doesn't sound like his voice.*

Suddenly the voices stopped and it became quiet. Then she heard footsteps slowly getting louder, coming toward her. Panicking, the adrenaline surging, she shone the flashlight around, trying to locate a hiding spot. Then she saw it, a small crevice on the side of the cave, just large enough to accommodate her undernourished body. She scraped herself into the crack, cutting the back of her hand on a jagged rock, wincing in pain, turned the flashlight off and waited, willing her heart rate to slow, her breathing to become less labored.

The footsteps stopped.

Black silence.

A short time later the footsteps started, getting louder, louder, until she felt the person right beside her, could almost feel his breathing. She heard the scraping sound on the ground as he stopped—she was sure he was right beside her but couldn't see him in the pitch darkness. She heard a click and recognized the sound. A safety lever on a gun being flicked off.

"Who's there?" Neanderthal Bennie Frost said.

Silence.

"I said who's there?" the grizzled tattooed ape said again. There was a moment's silence before he fired a couple of shots into the dark passage. The bullets ricocheted along the cave wall with a hollow pinging sound.

"I'll kill you if you don't announce yourself."

Seemed to Cadence, he would kill her either way.

Bennie marched away and the footsteps grew fainter. She could see the white luminescent dot of his flashlight beam unsteadily moving and then he stopped and it was silent again. The footsteps started again after a few seconds, growing louder.

Cadence flicked the safety on the semi-automatic Glock and waited. *Shit, he's coming back. He's going to see me.* Her palms were sweaty and she tightened her grip. *Only one chance. Make it good.*

Bennie's flashlight registered Cadence's glowing eyes just as she blinded him with a flashlight beam. The image in front of her wasn't Nathan and it wasn't Ed either, unless he gained about a hundred and fifty pounds. She doubted that as she pulled the trigger three times, one bullet penetrating Bennie's face through the bridge of his nose while the other two tore through his chest. The sound of gunshots in close quarters was deafening.

Falling back, he sprayed bullets into the rock ceiling before crumpling to the hard ground and breathing his last breath.

Cadence bent down to retrieve the dead man's weapon.

A slurred voice behind her: "Put that fucking gun down or get a bullet in the head."

She swung around shooting, too panicked to wait to see the intended target. *If he's with that other ape, he's bad news.*

But Arnie Jackman had already ducked and lunged at Cadence, winding her, sending her toppling backwards, landing on top of bleeding Bennie with a thud. She felt the sting of the butt end of a revolver as it smashed into her head repeatedly.

He's going to kill me, was her last thought as she lost consciousness.

Chapter Thirteen

Nathan was conscious of a gradual change in his friend. After returning from the near-death experience at the watery grave, Nathan had managed to find some bandages and some hydrogen peroxide, had cleaned and bandaged his own wounds.

But when he'd offered the first-aid kit to Ed, the man had only stared at him blankly, shaking his head slowly. Instead, Ed had pulled out some black shoe polish from one of the supply boxes, painted his face with stark lines and circles. On his chest he had smeared the shoe polish into the shape of a pentagram, a dark circle beside it, perhaps representing the moon. His face was a sinister mixture of black war paint, smeared with red blood from the small cuts the mutant birds had inflicted.

And, more and more during their conversations, Ed would go blank and stare silently at the fire, without acknowledging Nathan's comments. Nathan feared the worst—a slow descent into madness. Last night he had slept uncomfortably, tossing and turning, fearing that at any minute he would become the victim of an enraged assault by Ed. When he finally did fall asleep, he had dreamed the man was stabbing him repeatedly with a knife. He had bolted upright in the blackness, sweat-soaked and terrified, his heart pounding in his chest.

"Do you want some more tea?" Nathan finally asked as they sat around the small fire. He wouldn't dare mention the war paint as last night Ed had become irritated after Nathan kept telling him his wounds would become infected if he didn't clean and bandage them soon. After he had responded by saying, "Why don't you mind your own fucking business?" Nathan had wisely changed the subject.

The grim reality of their horrific existence was starting to take its debilitating toll.

Ed finally looked up at him and nodded, the faint flicker of recognition appearing and then disappearing instantly. Nathan nervously sprang up and filled his teacup, filled his own, and sat down next to the man who now resembled some kind of a demented tribal warrior.

He had briefly asked Ed some questions this morning when he awoke, trying to tweak in his own amnesiac mind the relationship they once had. *How were we connected? When did we become friends?*

But answers had not been forthcoming and now Nathan was convinced, failing a remarkable recovery from his amnesia, he would never know the relationship he once had with this man. He had thought if he could remember something, anything about what they had done together, he might have a chance at bringing Ed around, back to his normal self—whatever that was.

But it seemed the tragedies Ed had endured had finally taken a cumulative toll, rendering him numb to the suffering, numb even to the notion of survival. Although resembling a tribal warrior, he seemed to have lost the will to live, the will to go on fighting.

A faint scraping sound above snapped Nathan from his contemplation. Ed jerked his head alertly. Maybe he hadn't lost the will to live, at least not the will to fight?

Nathan stood up, moving closer to the sound. He reached the small entry hole leading up to the rock-sealed entrance they had descended, how long ago now? He didn't know. But he was sure the sound came from there.

"You hear that, right?" he asked Ed, whose head seemed to have cleared.

Ed nodded, flicked the safety catch from his machine gun and approached the hole. They listened silently. Slow, steady scraping, barely audible voices and something else—a muffled scream. The scream of a woman in trouble.

"Should we go up?" Nathan asked.

"Kill them all."

Flashlight in hand, Nathan scrambled into the entrance, digging his way up the water-soaked, muddy incline, Ed behind him silent but close. Halfway up, he remembered. *How are we going to get the boulder lifted? We're not strong enough for that.* He turned, shining his flashlight into Ed's vacant eyes. "We can't lift that boulder. It's the size of an armchair. We can't go up."

"I'll lift it."

"You can't. It's too heavy."

"I'll lift it."

"No, it's not going to work." An image suddenly flashed in Nathan's mind. He did remember something. An image of Ed working with tools. He was a carpenter. He distinctly remembered seeing Ed renovating a house, even helping him. The image of the house was vague and right now that was the only memory he had of his friend. Working on a house together, Ed's house.

"Hey, remember that time we renovated your house together?" Nathan improvised. "And that beer sure did taste good afterward. Didn't it?"

The same flicker of recognition. "It sure did," Ed said, smiling, the smile that Nathan remembered. "You remember."

"Yes," Nathan said, relieved to be getting some memories of his friend back, probably his only hope, however slim, of getting him to behave rationally. "Ed, think. Is there another way into the cave, another entrance?"

Ed was silent for a moment, the same blank stare beginning to envelope his war-painted and worn features.

Nathan grabbed him by the arms, shaking him.

"The ocean," Ed said, finally. "The birds."

Nathan thought the ocean route was far too dangerous, would put them in harm's way—expose them to the vicious killers roaming above, now probably occupying the cave, guarding the surface. "Anywhere else, Ed? You planned this for a long time. Think. You must know every inch of these tunnels."

Ed's eyes rolled back in his head and fear washed over his face. Nathan was also afraid—afraid Ed might turn on him at any moment.

"Your bedroom," Ed said finally.

"What about it?"

"There's a false wall of dirt behind it. An entrance. It leads to the main cave, the one we stayed in."

"Let's go," Nathan said. "Let's kill those motherfuckers, get some diesel and get this boat off the island. Newfoundland, our only hope."

"Kill those motherfuckers," Ed said, sliding down the small hole in front of Nathan.

A few minutes later they were peeling dirt off a wall with small shovels in Nathan's bedroom, directly behind the old mattress that was Nathan's bed. It seemed Ed in more cognizant days had thought out this intricate maze of tunnels rather intelligently. He had secret passages all over the place. It was now a question of keeping him sane enough to remember them. And keeping him sane enough so that he wouldn't turn on Nathan and decide to kill him.

Chapter Fourteen

I'll kill him. I'll kill both of them, Cadence thought as she watched her two attackers huddled over a small fire and drinking from a half-full bottle of Jack Daniels, bursting out into raucous laughter occasionally.

She was stripped naked, but for a torn pair of panties, her legs and arms tightly bound with ropes. She lay on the old mattress, eyeing the predators, trying to take her mind off the pain. Her vagina was sore and her head still ached from the pistol-whipping she had suffered at the hands of Arnie Jackman and Butch Belter.

She didn't want to think about it, was glad she was unconscious when it happened, but she knew she had been raped. Her eyes wandered across her bruised body and she saw for the first time red stains on what had once been white panties. She had no idea what injuries she might have down there from the vicious attack but she knew one thing. Her vaginal cavity ached and she suspected something was torn and damaged.

There were blood smears on her arms, legs, up her waist, and blood-smeared handprints on her shapely breasts, a grim reminder these scumbags had taken her roughly and ruthlessly. The only consolation she took was that she had not been conscious during the attack. They had had their way with her while she was unconscious, evidently finished before she had regained consciousness.

Butch Belter took a swig from the bottle and eyed her. He was about 250 pounds, cropped black crew-cut and small goatee. His face was pock-marked with acne scars. "Sleeping beauty," he said. "You're finally awake. Did you enjoy the romance last night?"

"How about a repeat?" Arnie said, grabbing the bottle from his partner in crime and swallowing a mouthful. "We've got booze."

"Fuck you!" Cadence said, imagining all the ways she would enjoy making them suffer.

"Wrong," Butch said, laughing. "No, we fucked you."

"Yeah, we fucked you good," Arnie said.

Cadence felt the goose bumps first on her aching feet, bound too tight and starting to turn purple from loss of circulation. Then, like a smattering of cold water from a lawn sprinkler, the bumps crawled up her entire body. She shuddered.

"How's your pussy feel, you fucking bitch?" Arnie said. "I gave you the big fucking stove pipe."

Arnie and Butch were too drunk to notice it but Cadence heard the sound, about four feet above and beside the mattress she was on. A pebble fell to the ground. A few minutes later, another.

The Neanderthals were oblivious in their drunken stupor.

A large section of wall fell away, exposing a hole about the size of a manhole cover. Butch and Arnie only had time to look up and drop their jaws before an AK-47 machine gun barrel and painted warrior emerged spraying bullets and yelling, "Die, you motherfuckers, die."

Butch managed to get a shot off with his pistol as he stood but he had already been shot about five times and was falling. His lone bullet ricocheted off the cave ceiling.

Arnie was sliced down by about a dozen bullets as soon as he looked up. They had learned the hard way. It didn't pay to drink on the job.

Nathan stared almost in shock at the teary-eyed, blood-smeared woman strapped to the mattress, her eyes widening as they approached. Ed had his gun pointed at her head.

"No," Nathan said, recognizing the face from his dreams, grabbing Ed's arm and directing the firing machine gun into the rock ceiling of the cave, bullets ricocheting off and zinging everywhere.

Ed's eyes had glazed over and he kept firing as Nathan tackled him to the ground. Struggling, they rolled around, Nathan grabbing at the machine gun, trying to wrest control of it from Ed.

"Stop it, Ed, stop it!" Cadence shouted.

There was momentary silence as Ed stopped firing, froze, and looked at Cadence. Nathan gripped the machine gun tightly, still trying to pull it away. Ed released his grip on the weapon. His faraway eyes returned to normal. "Cadence, is that you?"

"Get me out of here, please," she pleaded.

Ed stood up dusting himself off as Nathan rushed over to Cadence, extracted his knife and began cutting the constricting ropes. He stared into her eyes as he did, seeing immense pain and hurt deep within those eyes. The face was familiar but that was all. He still had no memory of his relationship with this woman.

"Nathan," she said, after she was free, wrapping her arms around him in a tight embrace and beginning to sob softly. "I knew you were alive."

Chapter Fifteen

He didn't deserve to live. He was better off dead, Velvet thought the next day as she trained her high-powered rifle with scope on the pile of debris about fifty feet in front of her. She was hidden in one of the piles in a makeshift cave, prostrate, waiting for the first attacker to poke his head up around the perimeter of her property. She had heard a vehicle approaching from the distance, fired up her diesel generator in the pit to distract the attackers, exited and resumed a guard position. Waiting, finger poised on the trigger, her mind had wandered back to the day she had killed her father, drowned him in the ocean and made it look like an accident.

He had started sexually abusing her from the very tender age of twelve. The abuse had started off infrequently, about once every few months and slowly escalated in frequency and intensity. Jeritt Jones was not a very nice man. The infrequent assaults turned to once, even twice a week. And they had become violent. A heavy drinker, he would fly off in a rage when her mother Margaret was at her government office job (Jeritt couldn't hold down a job to save his life), slap Velvet around a little, tie her to the bed and have his way with her.

It had gone on for fourteen months before she finally built up the courage to tell Margaret, who quickly dismissed the idea, accusing Velvet of being a "bad girl" and "making up nasty stories about a very decent man."

That's when she had plotted the Sunday afternoon boat trip. She had convinced Jeritt they would have much more fun "playing" on a boat in the ocean. They had paddled to a secluded cove, he had had his way with her in between tossing back beers. After he had finished, he had leaned over to pull another cold one from the cooler and she had pushed him overboard.

Every time he tried to surface, flailing his arms and screaming for help, she had plunked him under with the oar, until finally he had drowned. Thinking about it now, she smiled remembering the emotion she had felt as she watched him die—happiness and joy at finally being set free from his molesting clutches.

A board snapped in the distance and her smile vanished. She trained the scope on the intruder cresting the top of the debris pile, her perimeter fence, took aim and fired. A lone bullet penetrated his head and he dropped dead.

Another one appeared and she didn't waste any time, firing two bullets that tore through his head and smiling again as she watched him slump, roll down the debris mountain and lay motionless. *Fucking Neanderthals. Die, all of you.*

It was silent for a few minutes, but for the steady hum of the generator, wasting precious diesel.

She peered through binoculars, slowly scanning the entire perimeter. But for a rat that had poked its head out in the distance and scurried away, she could see no signs of her enemy. At least none that were among the living. She strained her ears, trying to hear the motor of the vehicle that had approached, that she couldn't see but knew was parked just beyond her sight lines, just outside of her makeshift fortress.

All she could hear was the steady drone of the generator and she wondered if it had been such a good idea to leave it running. Perhaps it was drowning out the vehicle's engine?

But, no, they would have turned the vehicle off already anyway, would've wanted to wait in silence while they attacked. Wouldn't they?

She made a snap decision to run for the other perimeter, where the sight lines were much better, where she could get an unobstructed kill shot.

She groaned as she rolled, got up. She didn't know how long she had been frozen in the sniper position but it had been certainly long enough that her body, balancing on jutting pieces of construction material, had begun to ache.

She quickly ran down the perimeter fence, sprinted along the ground in front of the barn, stopped momentarily to examine the dead attackers, and scrambled up the other side, peering out at the wasteland beyond. A black pick-up truck was parked below, two men stood outside dousing the debris with gas, another two inside the truck, evidently discussing something which could not be heard over the generator's drone.

Velvet, she preferred the nickname Black Velvet although she rarely mentioned her preference to outsiders, and almost everyone was an outsider to her, opened fire, striking one of the Neanderthals in the chest three times. He dropped his gas can and slumped on top of it. The other one raised an AK-47, these guys were well armed, and sprayed bullets at her. She ducked as a dozen or so zinged past. When she poked her head over a moment later, she noticed the perimeter in flames. The man had started it ablaze and jumped in the back of the black truck, which was now speeding away.

Black smoke swirled in front of her as the flames quickly began engulfing the perimeter. *Shit. I never thought of that. They're burning my protection, then they'll return to kill me.*

She aimed the assault rifle at the retreating vehicle, finally zeroing in on the back of a head. She fired one shot that blew the man's brains out and he slumped over dead.

She reloaded quickly, was about to blow the tires out on the truck, but the smoke had become too thick, the flames already too hot. She couldn't see her target anymore and her eyes watered from the toxic flames and smoke that rapidly advanced on her.

She scrambled down the hill, scavenged what weapons and ammunition she could from the dead men, raced into the barn and quickly tossed three duffle bags and a knapsack into her waiting pick-up truck. Living on the edge, she always kept survival and weapons packed up, ready to load up and leave at a moment's notice. In this new world order, she would not afford herself the luxury of slowly and methodically packing. Dawdling could mean death.

The wind had started to intensify in the late afternoon and she also knew fanning flames could leap over barren areas and ignite other areas if the wind, temperature, and the size of the fire were just right. She thought the conditions looked perfect for the wooden barn to quickly become a deadly flaming inferno.

And she was not prepared to venture into the pit, thinking it too shallow for surviving the blaze. Even if she did, she would be wide open to attack after the fire. And they would not stop now until they had robbed, raped, and killed her. And one thing Velvet knew for sure. No one would ever rape her ever again for the rest of her life, even if it meant killing herself to prevent it.

She started the truck, pulled out of the barn and stopped, feeling the intense heat before seeing a seventy-five foot high circular wall of flames, crackling, popping, belching toxic black smoke high into the crimson sky.

The truck in drive, she stepped hard on the brake and floored it, releasing the brake after the rear wheels started spinning and screeching, burning rubber, spitting gravel. The truck barreled toward the wall of flames, hit it with a crash and burst out the other side, flaming debris clinging to the front end, threatening to catch it ablaze.

Velvet slammed on the brakes, jumped out and, with yellow leather gloves, began picking off the burning debris. But an oil mixture had exploded on the hood, the result of plowing through an old oil drum and flames now covered the windshield.

She pulled open the door, feeling the flames singing her eyebrows, the sides of her black hair, which was now tied back into a pony tail, and pulled out a fire extinguisher, quickly dousing the advancing flames with the white chemical compound.

She climbed in and peeled away toward Montague and the Neanderthal hideout, which she had located on a recent scavenging mission. She had a single thought in her mind—revenge. *Fuck with me you're going to get it tenfold you bastards.*

She drove for about fifteen minutes, finally parking the truck behind a large pile of rubble which in better times could have been measured as a few city blocks away from the

Neanderthal hideout, or one of them at least, the one she had located. She didn't know how many hideouts they had, how many Neanderthals there were and she was hardly in a mood to start figuring it out now.

Her singular focus was to go on the offensive, knowing that to continue to operate in this defensive mode would mean a sure end to her life. It was only a matter of time.

It was dusk now, the rubble-strewn landscape illuminated by an orange and grey sky that was rapidly darkening, becoming more hostile and less visible. The wind whistled as she exited the truck, quickly reddening her pale white skin with its force and temperature. She flung the black scarf over her face, covering her nose and mouth, and pulled her baseball cap down over her head, leaving only a small area for vision.

Armed to the teeth and carrying a gas canister, she started walking and stopped suddenly. A crying sound to her left, soft at first and growing louder. She turned her head and saw a small leg protruding from some rocks and bricks, twisted wooden rubble.

She pulled some of the debris away, shone her flashlight down on a young girl who had become trapped and was crying for help. Her clothes were torn, her right leg badly crushed, still trapped under large boulders, her chest partially caved in. Who knew what internal injuries she had, how long she had been trapped there?

The girl, blonde matted hair, tearful eyes, pain-filled expression, focused on Velvet and said, "Kill me, please."

She had barely gasped the words and now labored to breathe, her only wish draining most of her remaining energy.

Velvet stared at the girl for a few seconds, extracted a pistol, fastened a silencer, aimed it and fired a single bullet into the young girl's chest. The girl smiled and closed her eyes, at peace finally.

"Rest in peace," Velvet said, sliding the pistol into a holster and carrying on.

A few minutes later, she was crouched behind a large rock near the partial building where her enemy stayed, eyeing a lone guard bundled up in a thick parka patrolling the headquarters.

As he walked passed, she jumped out, extracted a knife, approached him from behind and slit his throat.

"Aaaaaaaaaaahh," was all he said as he fell forward and died.

Velvet walked along the building and spotted the black pick-up truck a few feet away, also being guarded. This would be a little harder. There was no cover between her and the truck. She poked her head around the corner of the damaged hospital and was met with gunfire. *Shit*, she thought, diving out into the open, aiming the handgun and emptying the chamber.

The man advanced toward her, now limping after being struck in the leg with a bullet, but still firing, still coming at her. She tucked the piece into her holster, hoisted the machine gun and fired—rat-a-tat-tat, rat-a-tat-tat. A line of bullets penetrated the man's chest. He shouted, gasped, and dropped to the ground dead.

Footsteps, lots of them, could be heard scrambling up the basement stairs. She pulled out a grenade, popped the pin, and tossed it into the hole, which she believed to be the only exit. But she wasn't sure. The grenade exploded with a bang, rocketing debris into the sky as she stood, grabbed her gas can and ran around to the far corner of the building. *Shit. Why didn't I disable the truck? Because you didn't have time, that's why.*

She stopped and listened, could hear a man faintly barking out orders at another corner of the building. *It's now or never.* She quickly emptied the contents of the gas can onto a corner of the building, piled high with wooden debris, and set it ablaze with a match. *You light my home on fire I light yours on fire. How does it feel?*

She ran from the building, gunshots trailing her exit. She quickly glanced back, saw six, maybe seven men firing at her, some of them beginning to give chase. A few seconds later she scrambled up and over the pile of rubble where her truck was, crouched down and began firing at the rapidly approaching Neanderthals. The flames engulfed the building behind her, throwing an orange fiery light into the sky and illuminating the enemy. Sitting ducks. But, in this case they were running ducks, but visible ducks nonetheless. She had picked the pile of rubble because of its strategic location—no cover around its perimeter for more than fifty feet.

She pointed the machine gun and fired, waving it around and shouting, "Fuck you, fuck you" as she killed one, two, three of them. Two or three ran left, diving over a burned-out vehicle for protection.

A fierce firefight ensued. The building exploded in the distance and in the orange silhouette Velvet saw the black truck in motion, driving right toward her.

She slid down the hill, got in her vehicle and drove away. In the high winds, now freezing temperatures, she didn't know how long they would give chase. No one dared wander too far at night in this deadly environment unless they were stupid. *Like me*, Velvet thought, as she floored the truck and tried to put some distance between her and her attackers.

A shower of bullets bit into the rear tailgate and she winced as she jerked the wheel hard left, not wanting to give the Neanderthals a straight line in which to take aim and fire. *Keep the vehicle swerving, keep it swerving.*

Suddenly the pursuing vehicle was right next to her, two Neanderthals hanging out the windows, leveling their guns. Two bullets tore through the passenger door and Velvet slammed on the brakes, skidding the truck into a fishtail so fast she almost flipped it end over end.

She remembered a rock outcrop close to the hideout, gunned it in what she thought was the right direction.

Karl and Russ had overshot her by quite a distance, the momentum of their speed taking the black pick-up another two or three blocks before they finally stopped, fishtailed around, and resumed pursuit.

Now sand and dirt had whipped up, making it almost impossible for Velvet to see. But she floored it anyway, hoping against all hope there were no formidable obstacles directly ahead, praying, although she did not believe in God, that she could make it to the outcrop before they killed her.

Night now had its firm grip on the landscape and the clouds obscured the moon completely. She glanced in her rearview mirror and couldn't see headlights. *Did they give up?*

A few minutes later, the sandstorm let up, only for a moment, but enough time for her to see the outcrop of rocks just ahead maybe five hundred feet. She slowed, approaching from the left, knowing it would give her an excellent sniping advantage if she could enter from the left, park and scramble up the top of the hill. She would be able to pick them off from a distance if they hadn't given up chase.

She skidded to a stop, jumped out of the truck, scrambled forty feet up the rocky path, lay down in a sniper position and pointed her rifle, searching with the scope for the first sign of headlights. The sandstorm had intensified a little, and the bite of airborne debris striking her face along with the cold temperatures made her shiver as she scanned the darkness. *Surely the lights will be visible, even in the sandstorm. Let's hope.*

Chapter Sixteen

"What's the fucking point anyway? Do you think there's hope? There is no hope. We're all going to die," Ed told Cadence as she dabbed at his wounds with peroxide, cleaned, and bandaged them. On some rational level, she was the only person who had gotten through to him and he sat grudgingly while she played nurse.

She had just explained that they had a chance at a better life and that's when his eyes had narrowed, expressing his negative views about their plight.

"You always need hope," Cadence said softly, dabbing a cotton baton swab into the peroxide and wiping at a cut on his chest. "Hope is what keeps us going."

His eyes had gone blank again, so she continued working on her friend in silence. After her rescue last night, Ed had recognized fully the friendship connection and after she had dressed and composed herself somewhat, the three of them sat around the small fire, the two corpses slumped over beside them, a grim symbol of their precarious grasp on life and the terrible danger they were in.

They had discovered another full bottle of Jack Daniels, stoked the fire, and sat passing it around. Cadence had tried to enlighten Nathan, telling him various stories of how Ed, their friend and neighbor across the highway, had helped them renovate their Victorian-style oceanfront home to their tastes before they had settled in.

Apparently the three often hung out, going four-wheeling down the many trails and paths nearby their home, leisurely cruising on Ed's fishing boat, hanging out at the beach, or sometimes just sitting by a blazing fire at night, looking at the stars, talking and drinking.

Nathan, who sat by the fire now poking at it absently with a small stick, reflected on those stories and tried to make some sense out of them. Although he still didn't know her at all, remembering her fond look after they had rescued her made him feel good about having her at his side. Occasionally he would get fleeting glimpses of her smiling face, an image from some distant memory, but nothing would be attached to it. No context in which to slot it in his mind and categorize it.

But, he had to admit she was very attractive and had the traits he looked for in a woman. He tried to retrieve what he thought was some overriding negative emotion connected to the relationship, but other than a feeling, there was no concrete memory or memories associated with this wave of negativity that supposedly had something to do with her.

Cadence turned her head and smiled and Nathan forced a smile, trying to will away the negativity that was starting to creep into his mind. *Does it matter now anyway? If something did happen in the past, does it matter?*

Last night, they had slept huddled together in Nathan's Flintstone-style bedroom. In the middle of the night, or day, he didn't know anymore, he had awoken to small sobs coming from this mysterious woman. He touched her arm gently and she had cringed, evidently still struggling with the trauma of the violent kidnapping and rape. *Whatever you do, don't ask her now. Give her time to heal.*

"We have to get rid of these bodies," Nathan said. "They're going to start rotting."

Ed gripped his weapon at the verbal intrusion and Cadence gently touched his arm. "Now, now, Ed. He's only talking. It's Nathan, remember?"

His fingers slowly loosened and he released his hand, letting the AK-47 lean against the plastic lawn chair while she continued.

"What are we going to do with them?" she asked, grimacing. "They're too heavy to drag up to the entrance and we'll never get them into the hole through the upper quarters and then down to the ocean."

Nathan was thinking of other things at the same time. With the cave entrance compromised and now living back in the original bunker, they were exposed to attack. He knew it was only a matter of time before the Neanderthals came a knocking—knock, knock, knocking on hell's door. They would soon be looking for their comrades. He had another idea. "Why don't we seal off this hole after we get up to the other section, leave the bodies here? If The Neanderthals come, we can only hope they don't discover it. Stay one step ahead of them."

"I say we fight to the death," Ed said, his vacant stare evaporating, madness and anger growing in his eyes, in his assaulted soul. "We're dead anyway. Let's go out with a bang, not like a bunch of cowards running and hiding."

Nathan had to admit, for someone who possessed an extremely precarious grip on his senses, the plan didn't sound that bad. At least it was bold, courageous, and proactive, which was more than he could say for his own plan.

A large explosion rocked the cave entrance far above them. Ed leaped off the chair, accidently shoulder checking Cadence, sending her toppling backwards, grabbed his weapon and started firing into the darkness.

Nathan jumped up and steadied Cadence seconds before she hit the ground. *Fuck, for someone so skinny, I'm pretty damned fast. Must be the adrenaline.*

Nathan grabbed Ed's shoulder and was flung to the side. Cadence gripped his shoulder and yelled into his face, "Stop, Ed, stop. Hold up for a minute."

He stared wide-eyed but removed his trigger finger.

"Let's listen," Nathan said, retrieving his weapon and lying down, pointing it at the black hole. "Don't waste your ammo. Wait until you see something." He shone his flashlight in the black hole and they waited in silence, Ed now lying down, Cadence alongside tightly gripping his shoulder, whispering something in his ear that seemed to calm and mesmerize him.

All they heard was the thumping sound of their hearts. In the soft glow of the fire, Nathan could see Cadence's chest rising and falling, could hear her heavy breathing. *She must be petrified,* he thought as he fought to control his own heart rate.

It was Ed who appeared calm. His wild eyes had given way to an intense focus and he stared ahead, waiting for a sound. Cadence had stopped whispering and they waited and listened.

They heard faint footsteps before the voice. Indecipherable at first, it finally echoed through the tunnel audibly.

"Cadence ... Cadence ... Cadence."

She jumped up. "Don't shoot, that's Velvet, my friend."

Ed's eyes had become vacant again, his previous expression of concentration, sanity and focus abandoning him for the moment. Recognizing the signs, Nathan grabbed his hand. "Wait, buddy. That's not the enemy."

Slowly the image of Velvet came into focus, trudging along, the weight of an arsenal of weapons slung over her shoulder, slowing down her progress. She also carried two large red gas cans. She set the cans down as she entered the fire-lit cave. Cadence ran to Velvet and hugged her tightly, as she dropped her arsenal on the ground and metal clanked.

"You came back!" Cadence said. "I knew you would."

Velvet curiously eyed the others and Cadence made the introductions. Finishing, she said, "She saved my life after I escaped."

Shivering cold, Velvet sat down by the fire, explaining that her stronghold had been burned to the ground by the Neanderthals, how she had exacted her revenge, killing off a number of the violent tribe, burning their fortress and finally, how she had collapsed with exhaustion outside the cave last night inside her truck, waking a few hours ago to load her gear inside and blow the entrance, sealing it off from their predators, who were sure to return for revenge. She frequently glanced at Ed as she spoke, a look of distrust etched in her furrowed brow.

"Are you saying we can't get out now?" Nathan asked, looking to Ed for answers.

He only stared at Velvet blankly.

"We can't get out and they can't get in," Velvet said. "Would you rather I left the entrance open to invite those savages back?"

Nathan didn't know what to say so he said nothing.

"Don't you have another way out of here?" Velvet asked, searching the eyes now gathered around the fire. She leaped to her feet, drew her gun and pointed it at Ed, who had been staring at her uneasily, his finger sliding closer to the trigger on his machine gun.

"Get your fucking finger off that trigger or you'll get a bullet in the head," she said.

He raised the barrel of his gun at her head and smiled. "If I go, you go."

Cadence quickly grabbed Ed's sleeve. "Ed, she's our ally, not our enemy. Put the gun down."

The stand-off continued for a few seconds, the tension in the air mounting. Finally, Ed lowered his weapon, his eyes still fixated on Velvet, the same sinister smile remaining.

"What the fuck's wrong with him?" Velvet asked, taking a seat by the fire.

"He's been affected by this madness," Nathan said.

"Well get a grip," Velvet said, fixing a cold stare into Ed's eyes. "We start turning on each other we'll never get out of here."

The smile slowly disappeared from his features, a vague semblance of sanity registering in his eyes. "The boat. We can take the boat."

"A boat?" Cadence's eyes widened.

"Yeah," Nathan said. "There's a passage that leads to the ocean."

"But how did you get a boat?" Cadence asked.

"It's a long story," Nathan said. "Trouble is there's little diesel left." He didn't want to mention the killer seagulls yet.

"I've got fuel," Velvet said, pointing to the cans. "There's more at the entrance." She reached into her knapsack, pulled out a packet of cigarettes, took one out and lit it, taking a long drag and offering them around. Nathan and Ed lit up and Cadence politely refused.

Some calmness seemed to return to Ed's painted face as he dragged on the cigarette, blowing the smoke into the small fire, watching it swirl into the air as the heat from the flames fanned it up.

Nathan's head still smarted from the Jack Daniels indulgence last night but he thought the least he could do was offer their new guest and ally a drink. He fished around in one of the dead men's knapsack, producing another bottle of whiskey. He twisted the cap off and handed it to Velvet.

She reached for it eagerly and took a long pull, uttering an "aaaaaaaaaaahhhh" sound as she handed it back to Nathan. He took a drink and passed it to Cadence, who, more than happy to dull her senses a little, swallowed a few mouthfuls before passing it to Ed.

Nathan wasn't sure alcohol was the best thing for Ed in his volatile condition but nor did he want to exclude him. Ed had saved his life by bringing him down here. He owed him the benefit of the doubt. And, who knew how his mind would choose to process information if they could ever get out of this hellhole? Could he really blame Ed for his deterioration? Hadn't this new hostile environment changed all of them, really?

And, although he didn't know what kind of new terror might await them if they ever made it to The Rock, he was becoming sure of one thing every single day. That, to stay here would surely mean a descent into savagery and madness for all of them.

He shuddered at the thought, gestured for the bottle. As if sensing his thoughts, Velvet handed it to him quickly, her eyes searching his, trying to read his mind.

"I see you had a run-in with the scumbags," she said, waving to the dead bodies.

"Fucking bastards raped me," Cadence said, rushing over to the corpses.

Her eyes narrowed and her face twisted into a rage that Nathan had never before seen. Or, at least if he had, he didn't remember. She started kicking the corpse of Butch Belter hard in the face repeatedly, yelling, "Fuck you, fuck you, fuck you ..."

Nathan was about to stand up when Velvet placed a hand on his arm firmly. "Let her get it out of her system," she said.

They sat and watched her swear, yell, scream and kick dead people. When she was finally finished, both of their faces were pulp, unrecognizable. Arnie and Butch had seen better days. Her hiking boots and the cuffs of her blue jeans were splattered with blood. She walked over to Velvet who handed her the bottle of whiskey. She took a long pull, wiped the sweat from her brow, handed the bottle to Ed and sat down.

"Sorry," she said, burying her face in her hands. "I had to get that off my chest."

Nathan approached Cadence, put his arm around her, and kissed her gently on the cheek.

After a while, he sat down. *We better get out of here. And soon.*

Chapter Seventeen

"We better get her, and soon," Neanderthal leader Karl Mulligan said, examining the burned-out wreckage of Velvet Jones' pick-up, a charred remnant of what was once a reliable truck. He knew she had torched the vehicle so it wouldn't become part of the Neanderthal collection.

Russ stared inside the blackened cab trying to find evidence of human life, a skeleton maybe. "There's nothing in here, boss."

"Of course there isn't, stupid. She's in the hole and our two guys are probably dead," he said, pointing to the sealed-off cave.

The gang's former headquarters had been all but leveled by Velvet's handiwork with the gasoline, so they had moved onto her property, into her barn and the little mechanic's pit, which Karl had three of his goons working on, digging out a network of caves; a more reliable and secure fortress. It was no small miracle the perimeter blaze hadn't burned the barn into the ground.

But Karl had other plans. He planned on penetrating the cave, torturing its inhabitants, raping the women and eventually killing them all. Then he would have his men customize the network of caves to his tastes, maybe keep the odd bitch around to service his needs, and rule Prince Edward Island through fear and intimidation. He would have one law, and it would be a simple one: *Do what I say or die.*

Oh, and one more just for good measure: *Piss me off and die.*

"Let the bitch out," Karl finally ordered Russ.

Russ opened the door of the black pick-up, grabbed a fearful and partially-clad woman by the hair and yanked her out of the truck. She stumbled and fell face-first on the ground, rolling and finally coming to a stop on her back, glaring contemptuously at Karl.

What had once been a white t-shirt was ripped and smeared with blood, exposing an ample breast. The only other article of clothing she wore, a pair of denim cut-offs, was also torn all the way up the crotch, dirty and blood-stained. Her face was cut and bruised, both eyes blackened from blows. Her hands and feet were bound with plastic zip-ties.

Karl and the gang had kept Lila Vale around for a week, beating and raping her as the inclination arose.

But Karl knew eventually Velvet would surface and he wanted to send a message. Lila was the unfortunate messenger.

"You'll get yours, you fuck," Lila said, staring at Karl. "What goes around comes around and I know your day will come. And it won't be pretty. You'll be slowly tortured and killed, but not before suffering horribly. You'll experience pain like you never thought possible."

Karl kicked her in the face hard. "Shut your fucking pie-hole, bitch. Russ, drag her to the cave entrance, put a bullet in her head, or if you want, beat her to a pulp with your baseball bat."

Russ smiled, grabbed Lila by the hair and dragged her roughly to the rubble that was once the cave entrance. He propped her up against a boulder, reached for his baseball bat tucked away in the back of his pants.

He wacked her in the mouth hard. Two teeth and blood sprayed out. She grunted but grinned, raising her bound hands in front of her face and with both hands flipped a double bird. "Rot in hell, you fucking assholes."

"Brave in death, I like that," Karl said. "Finish her off, Russ."

The baseball bat came down so hard it jerked Lila's head to the side and her eyes rolled back in her head. Russ hit her another ten or twelve times for good measure. By the time he was finished her skull was caved in, her one-time good looks unrecognizable.

"Let's go," Karl ordered, noticing a flock of birds approaching, a large deformed pig grunting in the distance, scuffing his front claws on the dirt, the precursor to an attack.

Russ admired his handiwork for a second or two before turning around and getting in the driver's side of the idling vehicle.

As the seagulls formed a circle above, slowly spiraling to the ground below, the pig grunted and charged. The vehicle sped away and the raging animal gave up the chase, looked curiously at the mangled corpse, and then raised its head and squealed as the birds en masse descended and attacked the mutant animal.

"What's your plan, boss?" Russ asked a few minutes later.

"We'll be back with some explosives," Karl said with a wicked grin. "Their problems are hardly over. Their nightmare's just beginning."

Chapter Eighteen

What a nightmare, Nathan thought, his head throbbing with pain. *Imagine waking up in a post-apocalyptic nightmarish existence, your head pounding with a hangover.*

That's one thing he did remember, what it felt like if you overindulged in alcohol. Like he had last night, finishing off first one, then two, then Cadence discovered another bottle of Jack Daniels and the four had become totally wasted, sitting at the fire, the bloodied corpses just a few feet away, laughing and joking until the wee hours of the morning. Of the time, he wasn't certain, however, as they still didn't have any way of measuring time in their underground abode.

What else were they supposed to do? Cry about their plight? Where would that get them?

But he knew one thing. Waking up after tying one on, he felt like an old man. His body ached, and, getting up off the tattered mattress to relieve himself, Cadence still passed out and snoring loudly beside him, he had staggered a few times while making his way down the dark tunnel to the communal washroom, which was also beginning to stink to high heaven. Or was that high hell?

Finishing up and staggering back, overcome by the putrid stench, he had to force the vomit back down his throat, otherwise he would have become a walking, projectile-vomiting machine.

He couldn't decide if he was just edgy or still drunk as he shone the flashlight on Cadence, who had stopped snoring now and appeared to be sleeping peacefully, her long blonde hair covering half her face, her pouty lips pursed but closed, now breathing evenly and slowly from her nose.

But he knew his problems appeared much more real, and more stressful when viewed through a post-alcoholic lens. He held his hand in front of his face and noticed, not for the first time since he woke up, that it was shaking. He felt anxiety creep up into his head, a feeling of dread that he couldn't seem to shake. *Maybe I should have another drink? Hair of the dog to settle my nerves. No, better not. Tea maybe.*

He trudged down the dark tunnel to the main living area, trying to piece together the events of last night. Was it all good? He didn't think so, but he didn't remember the whole evening, didn't even remember making it to his bed. A partial black out. Not a good thing. Wasn't that the first sign, or one of the signs of an alcoholic, blacking out, not remembering events, things you said, things you did? *Did I say anything bad? Did I do anything bad?*

He didn't think so, but he wasn't sure. He would have to ask the question, the dreaded question. And then something did come to him in his haze. Ed freaking out. Yelling something about how he was going to kill everybody. Everybody? Didn't they finally have to restrain him physically, slap him in the face a few times to bring him out of his madness? Nathan thought so, the events of the night slowly coming back, exacerbating the feeling of dread. *Have to keep him off the booze. Never mind him, me too.*

However, Nathan didn't think of himself as the personality type that would be predisposed to alcoholism. That required an addictive personality, which he didn't believe he possessed. The other fortunate thing, he thought, was his system couldn't handle constant alcohol abuse. It would make him sick and he would be forced out of necessity to stay off it for a few days. He thanked God, if there was one, for blessing him with a physiology that couldn't tolerate excessive alcohol consumption daily.

Velvet had a pot of tea brewing on the fire as he walked in and sat next to her. She looked none the worse for wear, sitting pensively drinking her tea, her long black hair combed out attractively. She wore camouflaged green military fatigues and had an arsenal of weapons fastened to her. Her intense green eyes were clear, focused.

Nathan imagined he, on the other hand, resembled death warmed over, or worse still, death barbequed extra crispy. He knew he felt like it.

"How'd you sleep, sunshine?" she said, pointing to an empty coffee mug which he picked up and she filled with tea.

"More like passed out."

"Do you even remember getting to bed?"

"No."

"Cadence and I carried you."

"Oh."

There was a long pause. "Did I say or do anything stupid last night to, you know, offend anyone?"

"No," she said. "You're a happy drunk, unlike your buddy over there," waving to the tunnel that led to Ed's bedroom.

"I remember something about him. He freaked in a bad way right?"

"Yeah, and I don't trust him. He flits between sane and insane on a dime. Should we kill him?" she asked matter-of-factly.

"Kill him? No. He saved my life."

"Yeah, well you never know when he might decide to take it away. You keep a fucking eye on him then, because I'm not going to babysit his volatile moods 24/7. As far as I'm concerned, he's a liability."

What kind of a world was it when you could openly discuss killing somebody without fear of repercussion? Nathan thought. A world where your own survival meant not only fending off savage predators, but regularly looking in your own backyard to see if your neighbor, your friend, might be out to get you as well. More than just survival of the fittest. Survival of the smartest and meanest.

There was another silence as they sipped tea. Nathan glanced around the dimly lit cave, noticing the corpses, a few empty liquor bottles strewn on the ground, an old mattress a few feet from the corpses where Velvet had slept. There was something else, the gas cans were gone.

Velvet caught his gaze, seemed to read his hazy mind. "I took them down to the boat and the other ones too that were up there," she said, pointing to the tunnel leading to the main entrance.

Nathan was surprised she had already been working. But he was very glad to have this no-nonsense shit-kicking chick on his side instead of the other way around. He would hate to see what would happen if he crossed her.

"I started the boat," she said. "It runs okay. I think we should leave. And soon. The Neanderthals will not take kindly to all the men they've lost. They're going to be out for blood."

"Can you get us to The Rock?" Nathan asked.

"Yeah."

"Have you heard anything about it?"

"A friend of mine was slaughtered by Karl Mulligan. Brutally raped, tortured, and killed. She told me before she was captured The Rock was much further away from the blast zone than PEI. It's just hearsay, but there is no reliable information. Anyway, I don't see that we have a lot of choice. Do you?"

"I don't suppose we do."

Ed appeared from the small opening as they talked, looking disheveled but with a fresh coat of war paint on his face. He had black lines down both cheeks, a black nose and squiggly black lines on his forehead. He grunted, filled up a cup of tea, and sat down.

Cadence appeared a minute later. She glanced at the mangled corpses and Nathan watched her grimace with guilt or disgust, he couldn't tell. She looked tired but determined. He felt a well of emotion stirring. She was incredibly resilient to have survived this long.

She smiled weakly, poured a cup of tea, and joined them.

For a few minutes, Velvet led the discussion, outlining the merits of starting the boat and leaving immediately. Nathan and Cadence nodded when it came to the vote while Ed stared absently at the small fire.

"What do you think, Ed?" Nathan asked. "If we stay here were going to die for sure."

"Leave me here," Ed said. "I'll fight to the death."

"You heard him," Velvet said. "He wants to stay, let him stay."

"No, we're taking him with ..."

A thunderous explosion from above abruptly rocked the ground on which they sat. Their decision had been made for them. Velvet was the first to rise, pointing to some cardboard boxes of food she had packed. "Take them to the boat, Cadence."

Ed was right behind her but he wasn't thinking about packing supplies. He clicked the safety catch on his Kalashnikov—Nathan was surprised it was even on—shone his flashlight into the opening leading to the cave entrance, and disappeared. "If I'm not back in five minutes, leave without me," he said. "And sorry for the fucking up."

Nathan rushed around, grabbing supplies, throwing them into two knapsacks, checked his AK-47 to ensure it was ready to wage war. Less than a minute later, carrying weapons and supplies, he followed Velvet and Cadence down the tunnel leading to the boat, listening to undisciplined bursts of machine gun fire in the distance. Ed had evidently met with fierce resistance and a firefight had already erupted.

Just moments later Velvet had fired up the boat and the three waited on board while the motor chugged confidently.

"We should go," she said.

Cadence was busy packing away supplies for the trip out to sea.

"I'm counting down," Nathan said. "He's got two minutes."

Velvet was about to disregard the countdown and pull away, but at the last second, she removed her hand from the throttle and stood waiting while Nathan counted out loud.

"Two minutes ... 59 ... 58 ... 57 ... 56 ... 55 ..."

Cadence had finished packing away the survival items and stared at Nathan as a slow chirping sound began echoing through the cave, quiet at first but then growing in intensity, the fluttering of wings in tune with the chirping, which had now become a screech. Soon the angry mutant birds were swarming around their heads, bursts of machine gun fire punctuating their whistling attacks.

"10 ... 9 ... 8 ... 7 ... 6 ... 5 ... 4 ... 3 ... 2 ..."

"Let's go," Velvet said, throttling up the motor. "We're going to get eaten alive."

Cadence had gone below in the small one-bedroom cabin, protected from the winged attackers while Velvet and Nathan brushed them off and fired multiple rounds into the air.

Nathan nodded and she turned the boat around, gave it full throttle, weaving expertly around the narrow passageway to the ocean.

Ed, dressed in a grease-stained muscle shirt, half a dozen ammunition belts slung over his shoulder, had met with stiff resistance, moving through the dark tunnel toward his attackers. But he had a strategic advantage. He knew the cave like the back of his hand and he doubted his adversaries had the same knowledge. At the first burst of machine gun fire, he had ducked in a small crevice, behind a large rock outcrop that gave him a defense position from which to fire. And he knew there was only one way in. At least he hoped his attackers thought that.

After he had ducked into the crevice, narrowly avoiding the first round of bullets, he had sprayed a few rounds of his own into the blackness which was followed by some screams and shouts and the thudding sounds of bodies falling on the ground, dead or injured.

At least two. I've killed at least two. And there will be more, I promise you that much. If Ed had to be completely honest with himself, he would have to admit he vaguely remembered the events of the past week, or maybe two weeks he wasn't sure. He knew his descent into insanity wasn't quite complete, but it was close.

He remembered fleeting moments being with Cadence, Nathan, and Velvet but there were other large gaps in his mind, gaps of darkness in which the voices would tell him to kill everybody. And he had to fight to control them. Part of the reason he was here now, defending their escape, was that he thought it was the only place he should be, could be. At least here he was killing bad guys.

He had had many urges to destroy his friends, had come awfully close, closer than they would ever know, to acting on them. Last night, the insane voices driving him forward, he had crept into the cave where Cadence and Nathan were sleeping, approached the mattress, stood over them staring for a few minutes before finally extracting a butcher knife, leaning down, ever so close, bringing the blade closer, closer to Nathan's throat. It was only when Nathan coughed, rolled over, he had lifted the knife slowly up and some small voice of reason had announced itself in his head, saying *they're your friends, go back to bed.*

His head had cleared transitorily and he saw himself crouched over the two passed-out drunks, the knife held firmly in his hand, ready to slice the throat of Nathan King. He had blinked a few times, turned around and rapidly exited the cave, returning to his own domain quickly before the voices could return and send him on a murderous rampage.

Ed didn't know what had tipped the scales, sending him rapidly tumbling into the abyss of insanity. It could have been the beatings he had received from his father at a young age, or his mother always telling him he wasn't smart enough to ever hold down an executive job, or any job for that matter. Maybe it was because his mother always compared him to his sister, Emily, repeating with varying choices of words, "She's the smart one in the family. She's the one who will achieve great things in her life. You ..." and his mother would shake her head disapprovingly, often not completing the sentence.

So without proper role models, Ed had grown up with little confidence. Sure, he had graduated high school, but Emily had gone on to complete a PHD degree in business and economics and landed a job as an executive with a large oil company in Calgary. Ed couldn't exactly remember her title anymore, or even the name of the oil company. But he knew she made "six figures and then some."

His mother would never let him forget that.

After being fired from a half a dozen jobs, Ed had finally hung up his own shingle as a carpenter, saved up enough money to buy a few acres near Murray Harbor, and slowly but surely built his own house while he lived in a camper trailer beside the construction zone. His disrespect for authority figures meant he had a hard time taking orders from anyone and he had settled into a groove, contracting out his services. He knew he wasn't making six figures, maybe didn't have the brains Emily did, but he was very good with his hands, meticulous with his renovations, and his business was starting to grow.

He had even started a relationship, gotten married. But after two years, Melinda had moved out of the house, saying, "I can't take your mood swings." Shortly after, she had divorced him.

After she had left, his mood swings had grown worse along with his more frequent drinking binges. He remembered one time in a drunken anxiety attack, he had drunk-dialed a number of his friends and family, railing on each and every one of them. He wouldn't have recalled a single thing he had said, but he had made the mistake of also drunk-texting his inner circle. Reading the texts the following morning, he had to backtrack and make a number of phone calls apologizing, trying to salvage the relationships that, in a few drunken hours of anxiety, he had almost destroyed.

The content of his texts were nasty and threatening. To his ex-wife Melinda, whom he still referred to as his wife, *You didn't give me a fucking chance, so fuck you.* To his sister, Emily, *You think you're so fucking great. Well, you can just fuck off and die.* To his friend Nathan, *If you don't start returning my calls I'm going to come over with a 44 Magnum and put a bullet right between your eyes.* And another, *What part of fuck off and die aren't you getting?* To Cadence, *You're a fucking bitch like all women.* To his mother, *Don't fuck with me anymore. Fuck off!*

And on and on it went, sitting there in his house, going through his entire contact list on his smartphone, two o'clock in the morning, pissed to the gills, texting out nasty message after nasty message. A few hours later after the alcohol well had run dry and his head had started to clear, the horrific realization of what he had just done settling in with a dreadful finality, he had walked over to his gun rack, extracted the 44

Magnum he had promised to kill Nathan with, pointed it at his head and at the last minute had lost his will to die, instead crumpling to the floor, his hands covering his head, sobbing loudly, the fierce intensity of the misery reaching a painful catharsis. A few minutes later, weak from crying, in emotional upheaval, he had collapsed on the tiny throw rug on his living room, waking up in the morning with such anxiety and anticipatory dread, he thought of taking the gun again in hand to finish what he had started the night before.

Instead, he had cleaned himself up and made apologetic calls to all the recipients of the drunk-texting. Some answered, returned the calls and forgave him, including Cadence and Nathan, but others, including his mother, sister and ex-wife, had viewed the calls in a particularly dim light and severed any ties they once had with Ed.

One drunken evening. Half his inner circle wiped out. Priceless.

"Show your fucking face, you chicken-shit coward," Karl Mulligan bellowed down the tunnel, his voice echoing and reverberating eerily through the darkness.

Ed stared into the blackness. *Finish what you started, you chicken-shit coward.* "No," he said loudly to the voice in his head. "Before I go, they die."

Gunfire erupted again and bullets whistled past Ed's head, many ricocheting off tunnel walls and spitting sparks. The sound was deafening. In a flash, he jumped out into the tunnel, sprayed a few rounds and retreated back into the cave with the dead and mangled Neanderthals—the ones who had discovered the joys of disfigurement posthumously by meeting the boots of Cadence Whittaker. As he climbed into the small opening from which he had saved the life of Cadence, he began frantically piling up loose dirt, sealing his exit as the footsteps and voice of Karl Mulligan and the Neanderthals drew closer.

"I knew you were a chicken-shit. Run and hide, why don't you, but we ..."

The voice grew silent as he gathered the last of the dirt into place, the only visible evidence of his departure the barrel of the machine gun poking out and a small peephole from which he could see the enemy.

He watched the flickering fire. The suspended LED flashlight lamps provided an opaque window of light and maybe an opportunity to ensnare and massacre his bloodthirsty pursuers.

It was Russ Wiseman who entered first, a blaze of gunfire announcing his arrival. Then he stopped firing and shined the light frantically in all directions. He wasn't a calm or precise warrior.

Karl wasn't stupid enough to lead any attack. Let his followers die for him, not the other way around.

While Ed waited patiently, Russ shone the flashlight around the cave, stopped at the two dead bodies momentarily, then started waving the beam slowly across the walls.

Another Neanderthal entered and grunted. "You see anything?"

"Just a couple of bloody dead guys," Russ said, tension etched into his face. "Karl?"

He's waiting for the thumbs up, Ed thought. He wanted Karl more than anyone else but didn't know if he would be alive long enough to wait for his arrival. On the first flashlight pass, Russ had stopped momentarily at Ed's makeshift hide-out and Ed was just about to begin shooting when the other grunt walked in and distracted Russ from the fresh dirt.

Now he was slowly shining the flashlight again, and Ed could see the beam getting nearer to his eyes. Abruptly it stopped, blinding him for a second or two. "What's that?" Russ asked, pointing to the muzzle of the gun sticking out.

"I don't know," the grunt said, approaching. As he was about to pull it, Ed fired, grinning when he noticed the perfect row of black dots lining the man's chest as he moaned and dropped dead.

Russ started firing, but it was already too late. Ed leaped out of the hole, firing, yelling, "Die, you motherfucker, die." A row of black spots—that quickly turned red—appeared on Russ's chest, another four neatly patterned across his forehead and he dropped dead.

Ed jumped up from his crouched position but the big man was already upon him. Karl, hiding in the tunnel, watching the deadly events unfold, sprang out and with powerful force delivered a steel toe boot to his temple, sending Ed toppling back and crunching into the rock wall.

He grunted as Karl leveled his pistol and took aim, crack, crack, crack, three shots but no penetration into flesh or bone. He missed.

Ed, clutching his machine gun, rolled along the ground as Karl tried to kill him. But, in the sparsely lit cave it was difficult to see the target, his eyes still adjusting from the blackness of the tunnel to the LED flashlights and small fire.

Ed sprayed bullets.

Two ripped through Karl's right arm. "Oh fuck." Karl dropped his weapon.

It clanged on the ground as Ed withdrew a knife and flung it at his attacker. It sliced into his shoulder Karl winced, pulling at it with both hands as Ed leveled his AK-47 and opened fire again.

But Karl dove to the ground and was now crawling toward his prey, reaching his machine gun as he crawled along. He picked up the weapon. He hesitated only briefly to pull the knife from his shoulder, aimed the weapon and fired.

Ed had plenty of time to see the attack and kicked the machine gun hard. Bullets flew everywhere as Karl struggled to grasp the weapon's trigger again. Ed stood up, kicked Karl in the head, pulled the machine gun from his grasp and flung it away.

"It's your turn, motherfucker," Ed said, leveling the machine gun. *Ah, hell, one more kick in the head won't hurt.*

He kicked Karl hard in the head, slicing open a large gash above his eye. He enjoyed the sight of blood squirting out. *Like a geyser.*

Ed returned his finger to the trigger and prepared to end this man's life. Karl reached into his sock, pulled out a small handgun and fired two shots into Ed's chest. Ed looked down at the blood flowing from his wounds and smiled. *My turn I guess.*

A flashlight beam from the small entrance tunnel distracted him for a few seconds and he looked up. Two more bullets ripped into his chest and he stumbled back, switching the machine gun to automatic, aiming at the flashlight beam. He heard a grunt, the thud of a body hitting the ground, saw the flashlight drop, casting circular white patterns on the cave wall as it rolled along the ground. *Got him. The white light. I see the white light.*

Backing up, Ed slammed into the wall and withered down it, continued firing, spraying bullets in all directions. He felt his heart rate slow, his head grow dim. *This is what it's like to die. I'm dying.*

Ed listened to his slowing heart rate as the thoughts in his mind became muddled. His eyes wide open, he felt overwhelming darkness slowly envelope his soul.

And with a smile on his face, Edward Sole slowly exhaled his last breath and died.

Chapter Nineteen

"What're you talking about? Do you want to die?" Nathan asked Velvet as she navigated the diesel-powered fishing vessel along the shore line. It swayed violently in rough waters. The predatory birds had finally left them alone about five minutes ago and Nathan had stepped on deck after comforting Cadence, who was still huddled fearfully in the lower sleeping compartment.

Velvet's face, barely visible through the black baseball cap pushed over her black-rimmed sunglasses, was pock-marked with V-shaped incisions that dribbled blood down both cheeks. She put a hand to her face, wiping away some blood and smearing it along her cheek. It almost resembled rouge, but it wasn't her color, much too red.

She had explained to Nathan that she had to make a quick stop at her coastal property to retrieve a few things. When he had pressed her on the matter, she had finally come clean. She wanted to retrieve a photo of her thirteen-year-old daughter, Lisa, and a large box of old dynamite sticks and ammunition just in case they met with resistance at sea or when they arrived at The Rock. Apparently Lisa had either been killed in the initial blast or attacked and killed by the Neanderthals or other opportunistic savages. Who really knew how many tribes were out there, raping and killing for food or just for the fun of it.

"I'd like to get those things," she said, navigating the massive waves, glancing briefly at the grey mass of clouds that had rolled in, the sun silhouetted a dim orange behind the threatening sky.

"Shouldn't we vote on this?" Nathan said, observing for the first time a humane side to this mysterious woman.

Velvet paused a moment as a strong gust of wind rocked the boat sideways. She gripped the helm and Nathan firmly grabbed a rail with both hands while he waited for the gale-force wind to subside.

"Take the helm," she said. "I'll go and get Cadence."

Nathan took over and tried to steady the boat along its course. Velvet went below deck, returning a few minutes later with Cadence, who was nodding her head in agreement.

"Are you sure?" Nathan said. "It might be burned to the ground. The entire area could be occupied by Neanderthals."

Cadence brushed her long blonde hair away from her eyes. Strands of it were matted to her cheeks and it was obvious she had been crying. "That photo represents the only memory Velvet has of the person who meant the most to her in the whole world," she said, pulling the hood on her blue parka up over her head to offer a modicum of protection against the unyielding elements. "For better or worse, I'm prepared to take that chance."

"You okay with it?" Velvet asked Nathan.

Nathan nodded while Cadence returned to the cabin. "Give me a holler when we get close," he said. "Unless you need me here now I'm going below deck for a bit."

She shook her head and he disappeared inside the cabin, sat down next to Cadence on the small bed. "How are you doing?" he asked.

"I'll be okay," she said, pulling her tear-soaked hair back off her face and fashioning it into a pony tail, which she wrapped neatly with an elastic band.

He wasn't sure what to say.

"Is there something going on inside your head that I don't know about?" she asked, taking Nathan off guard.

There was something but he wasn't prepared to discuss it right now, unless of course she brought it up. "What do you mean?" he asked, stalling.

"Well, the way you look at me."

"How do I look at you?"

"Distrustfully. Do you remember anything at all about our relationship yet?"

"Is there something I should be remembering?"

"Nathan, I'm just asking you. Please answer me honestly."

"I remember your smiling face. I remember how you look when you're mad. I don't remember much else." After a long pause, Nathan stared directly into Cadence's stunning blue eyes and said, "But there is some overriding negativity that I can't put a finger on and it bothers me to no end that I can't remember it. Did something really bad happen between us, something really major that would shatter our trust and drive us apart? Because if there is, I want to know. I've noticed in the last few days I've been drawn to you more and more, like I'm falling in love with you for the first time and I don't want anything to get in the way of that. If there is something that would prevent us from moving forward please, please Cadence, I'd like to know."

He could think of a lot of things that would prevent them from moving forward, most of them completely beyond their control.

Cadence put her arm around Nathan and kissed him full on the lips. He felt the stirrings of desire growing. Cadence had been so traumatized by her brutal rape that Nathan, over the last few days, hadn't dared try to make any sexual advances. And she hadn't exactly instigated anything either so he figured in due time maybe she would heal, mentally and physically, and they could resume some of the carnal pleasures they must have enjoyed in the past.

An image of Cadence's desirable nude body popped into Nathan's head and in the image, he saw her clearly, gazing into his green eyes, smiling, writhing with pleasure. And in those eyes, he saw a deep desire. And love. He was convinced it was not his imagination. It was a memory.

She was about to begin and he stopped her with a hand to her lips. "I just remembered something else about you."

"What's that?" she asked anxiously.

"I remembered how amazing it was making love to you."

She hugged him and smothered him with kisses.

"You're not going to say anything to dispel those pleasurable memories, are you?" he asked.

There was a long pause again. "Do you want to know or not?" she finally asked.

"Tell me."

"The only way I can say this is to blurt it out."

"Go for it."

"You cheated on me. I was so hurt that I took my revenge by cheating on you."

"I did that to you?"

"Yeah," she said, a frown beginning to crease her full lips.

"Who did I cheat with, and who did you cheat with?"

"Is that really important now?"

Nathan thought about it a few seconds and finally said, "No, I suppose not. I guess the other important thing to ask is can you forgive me?"

"Yes. Can you forgive me?"

In this frightening existence that held out very little hope for a better life, what options were available to him? Right now he only had two friends in the whole world. And, one of them, he felt sure now, he was in love with. "Yes," he said.

He traced her eyebrows gently with his finger, watched her eyelashes flutter closed, etched the tip of her nose, and then followed the path of his finger with his lips. His heart thudded with longing for her as he tenderly kissed her lips. Soon they were rolling around on the small bed, to the lolling of the boat, peeling each other's clothes off eagerly.

A few minutes after making love, they lay together in bed, looking dreamily into each other's eyes and kissing occasionally as they chatted about nothing in particular. The post-coital cuddle.

There was a loud knock at the door. "Get dressed, lovebirds. We're here. If you don't hurry up I'll join you," Velvet said. It wasn't missed on Nathan that Cadence smiled sexily at the suggestion. And, if he had to be completely honest with himself, it might be something he very well might enjoy.

They dressed and exited the cabin. Velvet had already tied the boat off to a small dock in front of what remained of her property. She had stepped onto the dock, examining what was left of her makeshift dwelling. The debris perimeter surrounding it had been torched to the ground, a small pile of black ash and metal, non-burnable rubble remained. The barn was intact.

Straddled with weapons, they stealthily crept to an outcrop of dead trees, large pines now stripped of life, outstretched branches twisting and pointing out at odd angles, ripped, ravaged and razed by the nuclear holocaust, a shadow of their former selves. They swayed dangerously in the wind, but offered some protection from the barn. In case it was occupied.

"Oh shit," Velvet said.

"What?" Nathan said.

"Look," she said, pointing off to the side. Parked near a small pile of scorched rubble, was Karl Mulligan's black truck, barely visible in the darkness.

Cadence's eyes widened at the threat. "Let me kill him."

"Wait," Nathan said, putting a hand on her shoulder and stepping in front of her. "No, I go first."

"Look," Velvet said. "We're not going to fight about this." She laid out a plan after explaining the ammunition case was buried underneath the table, the photo inside the case. The plan was to have her approach from the front, while Cadence and Nathan went to the back door. Velvet would shoot a few holes in the door, drawing attention to it, and step aside while Cadence and Nathan entered from the rear and gunned down the Neanderthals before leaving with the ammo. And photo.

A Neanderthal exited the front door, loaded a large wooden box into the pick-up truck, and returned to the barn.

"What about that?" Cadence asked, pointing to a grenade fastened to Velvet's belt.

"I don't know," Velvet said. "It might blow the whole barn up if it ignites the ammo. There's a lot of ammo there and it's not buried that deep. Let's play it by ear."

Nathan in front and Cadence trailing, they slowly crept along the decimated landscape, and stopped at the back door, flanking it. Nervously, they waited.

Velvet crept around to the front entrance. She ducked as a Neanderthal appeared with another load of gear. It appeared the Neanderthals were relocating to the abandoned mine shaft. He returned to the barn and she sprinted to the truck, ducking behind it and waited.

As he returned and threw another load into the truck bed, she crept up behind him and sliced his throat. He emitted a gurgling sound as he dropped dead. She hoped it could not be heard from inside the barn. The wind whistled and whipped and she prayed it would muffle the sound.

She approached the door, turning her AK-47 to automatic and fired, a dozen or so bullets ripping through the weathered wood with a crunching sound.

She immediately dove to the ground, rolling as bullets penetrated the wood and zinged over her head in all directions.

"Now," Nathan said. But something was wrong. Cadence had shoved him to one side, stepped in front of him and charged through the back door before he even realized what had happened.

He rushed in after her, firing. Cadence had killed four of them, riddled most of their backs with bullets before they even knew what hit them. Two more ran for the front door, but Velvet crashed through it and cut them down before they had a chance to open fire. She was awfully quick with her weapon.

Nathan and Velvet were sprawled on the ground by that time, shooting at the Neanderthals as they clamored for their weapons. They had been caught by surprise. Cadence stood in the middle of the melee and fired wildly, angrily yelling something incomprehensible to Nathan.

Slowly the gunfire ceased and the cries of the dead and dying grew silent.

"You guys okay?" Nathan said.

Cadence and Velvet nodded.

For a moment, everything was quiet, but for the blowing wind, now intensifying, threatening a deadly storm.

A hand with a handgun emerged from behind a tattered mattress that had been thrown haphazardly in a corner of the room. The hand squeezed the trigger and fired a single shot that penetrated Cadence's head. She moaned and dropped dead.

Nathan saw red. He stood up, picked up a baseball bat leaning against the kitchen table and charged for the mattress. More bullets rang out that narrowly missed his head. Velvet wanted to shoot but held her weapon silently, too afraid she would accidentally kill Nathan.

He pulled the mattress away and smashed the left hand that held the gun. The hand of Karl Mulligan. The gun flew out of his hand with the force of the blow and he withdrew it, grimacing in pain. But then he smiled and reached for the pin on a hand grenade strapped to his waist. Before he could get to it, Nathan swung the bat at his head with thunderous force and crushed Karl's skull, snapping his head to one side so fast it also broke his neck.

Nathan didn't remember how many more times he hit the man as his mind had gone completely crazed and blank. He only remembered feeling the firm grip of Velvet's hand on his shoulder and finally hearing her yelling, "Nathan, he's dead, stop ... stop!"

He turned and stared at her, his mind slowly clearing, noticing a lone tear in her left eye. She blinked and it slowly snaked down her face and she quickly wiped it away with a hand.

He ran to Cadence who lay lifeless on the ground, eyes wide open, blood dripping down her nose and into her mouth from the single fatal gunshot wound. He put his hand to her face and slowly closed her eyes, wiped the blood from her face and stared at it. Her lips were pursed up slightly, falling short of a smile. *Maybe in death, she'll be happier than trying to survive in this God forsaken nightmare,* he thought, putting his hands to his face and sobbing.

Velvet had picked up a small garden trowel, kicked over the kitchen table, and was busily digging at the loose dirt underneath. "We don't have a lot of time," she said. "Help me ... please."

Nathan wiped the tears from his eyes and, picking up a small shovel, joined her. A few minutes later, the shovel punctured wood and Velvet leaned into the shallow hole and wiped the dirt away with her hands. "Grab an end," she said, pointing to a rope handle.

They hoisted the heavy wooden box up and set it on the ground. Velvet was about to pry the lid open with a large machete she produced, but abruptly stopped and listened. "Did you hear that?"

Nathan at first could only hear the unnatural howling of the wind, but then he did hear it. The sound of a vehicle engine far away, growing louder as it neared.

They had unwelcome guests.

"Let's go," Velvet said, pointing to the back door, the shortest distance to the boat.

They hoisted the box, slowly lugged it to the rear exit, the engine noise now highly audible at the front of the barn.

"Can you take it?" Velvet asked as they stepped outside to the sound of doors slamming and voices. She glanced at the grenade she had lifted from the dead body of Karl Mulligan, now fastened to her black belt. She glanced again at the red gas cans, strewn in the corner of the barn a few feet away from the body of Cadence, and Nathan instantly knew what she had in mind.

He was hoping for a dignified burial at sea for Cadence but now they had no time for that. Velvet planned on giving her a fiery funeral and roasting a few Neanderthals in the process.

Nathan nodded, and with strength he never thought he possessed, hoisted the box up and onto his shoulder. He slowly trudged along, feeling its weight, the corners piercing into his flesh. *Do it for Cadence. Do it for her. You don't know what those sickos will do to her body.*

As Nathan disappeared into the grey and crimson light of dusk, Velvet pressed herself to the side of the door and waited. *These goons are stupid*, she thought as four scumbags entered the barn, pointing their weapons cautiously around the macabre killing grounds.

"Someone check the back do ..." someone said, but didn't get a chance to finish the sentence.

Velvet pointed her machine gun inside the door and with a burst of gunfire killed the man and another standing next to him. The others started firing but she had already pulled the pin on the grenade and tossed it on the gas cans.

As she ran toward the boat, the barn exploded and a large fireball leaped into the air with a whooshing sound as it breathed and began its wooden feast. She looked back, saw and heard Neanderthals dying inside. One, engulfed in flames, ran out the back door screaming, wandered aimlessly in circles for a few seconds and then dropped to the ground, a human fireball writhing and twisting to a slow, gruesome and painful death.

Velvet smiled as she caught up with Nathan, grabbed a rope handle on the box and relieved him of half of its burdensome weight. "Those fuckers got what they deserved. But there may be more, let's go."

Nathan glanced back as they dumped the box on deck and Velvet fired up the engine. The flames were huge now, licking maybe fifty feet into the sky, engulfing the old wooden barn rapidly, black smoke spiraling up into the unwelcome sky above.

Velvet smashed the buttstock of the machine gun into the wooden box, cracking the lid just enough for her to pry it open. Just as she retrieved a rifle with laser night scope, a Neanderthal appeared in the small path, charging toward the boat, shooting. They instinctively hit the deck as bullets whizzed past them.

Velvet trained the laser sight on the attacker, steadied the red beam on his forehead, fired and blew his brains out before he could get within fifty feet of the boat.

"Nice shooting, Tex," Nathan said, as she jumped up, took the helm and revved the boat away from the dock, cruising out to an unknown fate at sea.

Chapter Twenty

Two days later the sea was calmer as they floated along in the hot mid-afternoon sun with no sign of land in sight, their fuel supply nearly empty. Nathan had a small bucket and was making return trips to and from the bilge, dumping out water they had taken on during the storm.

Velvet was at the controls, still trying to find The Rock. The boat had almost capsized after they had left PEI as nasty gale force winds had blown in. It had been battered by fierce high waves and pelted with rainwater from a torrential downpour.

Velvet had managed to save the vessel, but the storm had prevented her from keeping her course. Now, they had passed The Rock and had to re-chart the course.

Nathan returned to the deck with a bucket of water, dumped it into the ocean, littered with dead fish, and glanced at Velvet. For the first time since their departure, she held the picture of her daughter up, glancing at it occasionally as she navigated to where she thought The Rock might be.

"Is that Lisa?" Nathan asked.

"Yeah," she said, continuing to stare straight ahead.

"Can I see her?"

"It's none of your business."

He stepped onto the ladder leading to the bilge. "Sorry."

"Wait."

He stopped. She had finally turned around and was now looking him straight in the eye. She held out the picture. He thought he saw her eyes watering but if he did, she was hiding it very well with a hardened battle-weary expression.

He walked over, took the tattered color photograph and studied it. In it there was a cute bright-eyed black-haired girl sitting on a bicycle smiling cheerfully and innocently. She had stopped on a path leading out of the forest, which was in the background, large green deciduous trees. It was a bright sunny day. You could tell by the eyes she was enamored with the photographer.

"She's cute," Nathan said, unwilling to pry into the nature of the mother-daughter relationship. He could tell by Velvet's demeanor there was a lot of pain associated with her memory of this little girl and he didn't want to rub salt in a fresh wound, especially one that perhaps had scabbed over and was beginning to heal. "Who took the picture?"

"I did," she said. "I was with her just before the bomb."

Nathan had also heard a story about the Neanderthals killing Lisa and did not want to open up that can of worms either—even though they were at sea. So he just said "I'm sorry" and returned to the bilge. There was a lot of water yet to bail out.

But, filling the small bucket below, his mind began wandering again and he became absorbed in his thoughts. On one hand, he wanted to know more about Velvet's story, about which she had remained tight-lipped. On another hand, he wasn't ready for more tragedy. He had had his fair share of it in the last few weeks, or however much time he had spent in the caves in PEI. He didn't remember.

But he *was* starting to remember a few things. The evening they had embarked on their journey to who knew where, a few hours after Cadence's death, battling the fierce waves, taking turns at the helm, a flood of memories had washed over

Nathan's troubled mind. He remembered Cadence, their relationship, how they met, the good times, intimacy, and good memories they had shared. But the memories had only made it harder to come to grips with her death, harder to understand how his only soul-mate could be snatched away from him so unexpectedly and untimely.

He had become consumed by his grief and for the last forty-eight hours had said little to Velvet, other than the mandatory conversations necessary for their survival. He had also noticed a change in her demeanor, a silent and focused resolve he had never seen before. Her expression had become somber, her mood dark, as if they were grieving for the same woman.

He had started to wonder to what level of intimacy the two had formed a bond, but in the end dismissed the thought as trivial and meaningless, in light of Cadence's death. Did it really matter now anyway? Would becoming obsessed with it change anything? So he pushed the thought away and had tried to develop the same focused and steadfast resolve as Velvet. She was a survivor whom Nathan knew had endured extreme hardship and suffering. It was etched all over her face, visible in her eyes, entrenched in her personality and manifest in her attitude and actions. Nathan suspected the trust she had extended had been betrayed many times and she had formed an exterior coat of steel armor which was perhaps impossible to penetrate and had served her well in this battlefield. She did not let emotion cloud judgment. But she was not a machine either.

She had a few chinks in the armor. And, although few and far between, they showed him a part of her that he liked and identified with. She was a woman with an edge, a tough warrior with an iron will to live, but she was also capable of acts of kindness and humanity that he would not have given her credit for when they first met.

He had initially taken her suggestion to kill Edward Sole as ruthless and cold-blooded, but was it really? Wasn't Ed's precarious grip on sanity putting all of them in jeopardy? How close had Edward come to killing them? In the 1945 Battle of Iwo Jima, didn't Japanese officers kill their subordinates for what they viewed as unpatriotic acts? And Ed's behavior had been much more dangerous than unpatriotic. He had threatened to kill them, and his vicarious grip on sanity suggested he just might have made good on that threat if they hadn't gotten the hell out of there when they did.

But in the end, Nathan realized, there was some rational part of Ed that had prevailed and he had made the decision to fight the Neanderthals off while they made their escape. If it wasn't for him, maybe they'd all be dead right now. He wanted to remember the positive traits about his friend, knowing full well you never love everything about your friends all the time anyway. He was convinced Ed was dead but he also took some consolation in the fact Ed had died a hero.

And Cadence. Hadn't she died a hero also?

"What're you doing?" Velvet said, watching him stare at a small puddle of water in the bilge, holding a bucket full of water. "Throw that overboard. I need you rough and ready, up here. Stay frosty, will you. Now's not the time to wallow in self-pity."

Nathan stared up at the cold eyes giving him orders. He still couldn't remember certain aspects of his personality but he seemed to remember not being too fond of being bossed around. But he was in no mindset to protest. His survival depended on a certain amount of respect for this woman. He had to learn to like her and get along with her if he was ever to get out of here. And, he knew even that wasn't an assurance his life would last much longer.

"Someone coming?" he asked. Other than a brief attack by some mutant seagulls, which were quickly erased with machine gun fire since they could see them coming for miles, they hadn't encountered any signs of life on their two-day voyage.

"No. I see land. The Rock, I think."

Nathan scrambled up the ladder, reached the deck and looked toward where Velvet was pointing. He saw a rough and rocky coastline in the distance and could barely make out a small white two-story turn-of-the-century Victorian-style home perched on a boulder, a few white objects that appeared to be boats strewn in front of it and nothing else. No trees or vegetation of any kind. Rocky, barren landscape. Uninviting? He didn't know. But they were going to find out.

"How are we going to anchor there?" Nathan asked, surveying the steep and rocky cliff leading up to the house.

Velvet was viewing the terrain through a pair of binoculars. "Here," she said. "Take a look. There's a small sand spit sticking out, and it looks like a kind of path leading to the home, weaving in and out of the rocks."

Nathan peered through the binoculars and recognized what she was talking about. "Do you want to ground the boat on the sand spit?"

"No, drop anchor in the shallow part of the sand, walk through shallow water to shore. What choice do we have? We can't drop anchor further out. We'd have to swim ashore and I'm not doing that with all our ammo. I'm not leaving it on board."

Nathan realized she had thought it through and nodded. He readied to drop anchor as they chugged along at 12 knots, slowly approaching the small sand spit, the formidable cliff looming larger.

Dusk was just beginning to take hold, their fuel near empty. They couldn't have arrived at a better time. That's what Nathan thought anyway. He didn't know he would soon be regretting that thought.

"Now," Velvet said, a few minutes later and Nathan dropped anchor in the sand spit. A bank of dark grey clouds had just rolled in and the weather had turned forbidding. They packed some essential firearms, two water bottles, some packaged energy bars, their staples for the last two days, and after tying off *Delilah Blue* on a large rock, flashlights in hand, began the trek up the winding path to the white house.

Nathan alertly glanced around while they walked but saw no signs of life. Velvet was frosty also, pointing the AK-47 ahead, her finger massaging the trigger, the safety catch off. They reached the small house, sitting as pristine and undisturbed as it had appeared from a distance. There were four small fishing boats strewn on the rocks, the oars neatly tucked under the overturned boats, only the handles visible. Like someone had neatly stored their small crafts after a fun day of fishing in the ocean and were now sitting inside roasting marshmallows by the fire, enjoying the ocean view.

They arrived at the wooden yellow door to the house, both instinctively pressing themselves against either side, guns drawn. Velvet knocked on the door, removed her hand quickly in case someone decided to welcome her with gunfire. They waited in silence for a moment.

"Anyone in there?" Velvet said. Nothing.

"We mean you no harm," Nathan tried. "We need food, shelter." Nothing.

Velvet tried the door handle. The door squeaked open and she entered like a swat team member, stealthily and poised for attack. Nathan followed and she waved him into the kitchen while she proceeded up the stairs. She returned a little while later, shaking her head, giving the thumbs up all-clear signal. He acknowledged the signal with a nod and thumbs up.

The house was empty. Two dated floral couches were positioned around a wood-burning fireplace, chopped logs stacked neatly beside it. Two end tables at either end of the couches with Victorian-style lamps and a coffee table with a white doily sat in front of both couches, an assortment of plastic flowers in a vase in the middle. Some framed photos hung above the mantle of a couple with their three kids. The photos chronicled the lives of the family from early adulthood to old age. Everything was neat as a pin, if a little dusty. It looked like grandma's house, one of the small armchairs by the fire still fitted with thick clear plastic, making you think twice about wanting to sit in it for fear of damaging it or creasing the pristine plastic.

Nathan ran his index finger along the coffee table, leaving a line as it cut through the coat of dust.

Velvet was looking at the family photos on the wall.

"Weird," he said. "Like they just disappeared."

"It's home for now," she said, walking into the kitchen and rummaging around. She returned a few minutes later with two cans of beans, two oil lanterns, and a bottle of wine. "We have supplies."

Nathan busied himself at the fireplace and soon had a respectable blaze going, throwing a comfortable warmth into the otherwise chilly room. While they had no power or water, they at least had a warm roof over their heads and some food and drink, no small miracle considering their situation.

Using some fishing line, Velvet jury-rigged an AK-47 to the front door—set to fire if anyone attempted entry.

Mesmerized by the flames, by the soft glow of the flickering oil lanterns, Nathan sat on the couch and shoveled dollops of beans into his mouth while Velvet sat on the plastic-coated armchair by the fire, stoking it between mouthfuls of beans and sips of red wine.

And suddenly, as if the dam burst, memories began flooding into Nathan's head. He remembered working as a journalist, reporting on the daily happenings in PEI. It seemed to him things had been going well until he had overleveraged himself with real estate acquisitions. The three duplexes he had owned began having problems cash-flowing. Delinquent tenants, he specifically remembered Tyrone Clipper, *I hope he burns in hell*, had gotten the better of him financially and Nathan fell behind on his mortgage payments. That's when he started to over-indulging in alcohol, only compounding his financial situation. Too proud to tell Cadence, he had tried unsuccessfully to rectify the situation on his own, but it had only worsened.

And the proverbial straw that broke the camel's back was when he had received a $14,000 tax bill in April after his accountant had compiled all the numbers. Since he was a freelance journalist, he essentially contracted out his services and had to pay his own taxes. Problem was, he never put aside the money he needed or made quarterly installments to lessen the severity of the year-end tax blow—a debilitating shot to the liver.

It was around that time, he remembered, when Cadence was in Halifax on a business trip, that the sexy twenty-four-year-old cashier at Tim Horton's in Montague had asked him what was wrong while he purchased a coffee, a ritual whenever he found himself shopping in the small town. One thing led to another and that evening after a few bottles of wine he had taken Lila Pierson up to the bedroom he shared with Cadence and had his way with her, trying to lose his problems in carnal pleasures.

The next morning he had remembered being overcome with guilt as he had dropped Lila off in front of her small apartment in Montague. Exiting his car, she had winked and smiled, saying, "We'll have to do this again."

He had only nodded, but had no intention of repeating the performance. What was he, stupid? He loved Cadence Whitaker, the one woman he felt really understood him. That afternoon, arriving home, she instantly sensed something was wrong. She wondered why the sheets were freshly laundered and could see in his eyes that he had betrayed her trust, loyalty, and love. He didn't bother lying about it. There was no point. She just knew.

An argument had ensued, Cadence had broken down in tears and ran into their bedroom, slamming the door and sobbing.

It was only a few hours later the pitched roof on the old home had begun leaking water into the kitchen as the rain began pelting down. Not wanting to see the hurt he had inflicted on Cadence, he had left the house, retrieved a ladder from the barn, and climbed atop the roof, trying to determine the source of the leak. It was then that he lost his footing, slid down the slippery slope, fell the twenty or so feet and landed on his head, knocking himself unconscious and concussing himself so severely he had suffered amnesia.

And he had woken up on a tattered mattress in a dark and cold cave skinny and dirty, starving with hunger with no idea who or where he was.

Now, piecing together the events of his existence, he realized he had learned the hard way about why you should not commit infidelity. Hadn't they been together for three years, planned to marry, save their money, retire early and spend six months of the year in the Caribbean? He thought so.

And his preoccupation with money. Had any of it really made any sense in the context of his new existence? Wasn't it far more important to cherish the bonds you made instead of shamelessly pursuing material gain? Wasn't it ultimately the pursuit of money that had created this nuclear disaster he now found himself in? If it wasn't, it sure as hell played a big part.

What was he thinking anyway? Was he in competition with Cadence, a successful lawyer? Why wouldn't he swallow his stupid male pride, approach her and explain his financial mess? Surely, with her intelligence, they could have formulated a plan to get him out of it. He had learned a valuable lesson—don't let ego and foolish pride get in the way of a loving relationship. Money ultimately has no value when viewed in the context of the love he had for Cadence.

He set his empty bean can down on the coffee table, took a long drink of wine, refilled the cup and wondered if any of it really mattered now. Here, it was no longer a competition to outdo the Joneses, *oh right Velvet's last name is Jones, the Smiths then*, it was a fight for survival, shelter and food, the three things he had so easily taken for granted during his former, modern existence. He had it all but didn't realize it.

"Aren't you going to offer me some?" Velvet asked, waving an empty mug.

"Sorry," he said, walking over, refilling it and returning to the couch.

She stared at him now, the silence becoming uncomfortable. "Are you thinking of Cadence?" she said. She had removed her military jacket, washed her face with some bottled water in the kitchen and combed her long black hair out. Her tight black t-shirt accentuated her perfectly shaped breasts. She radiated an inner and outer glow, perhaps from the fire, or maybe it was just one of the many facets of Velvet Jones. Or maybe it was just the wine.

Nathan didn't know. But he knew one thing—she looked absolutely ravishing tonight.

"Yeah."

"You loved her?"

"Yeah."

She moved over to the couch beside him and stared into his eyes. "Can I tell you something about Cadence?"

"Go ahead," he said, starting to feel guilty after remembering the sordid details of his infidelity.

"I was very fond of Cadence too." There was a long pause. "We made love at my property, a day or so before she found you."

Nathan thought the news would hit him like a ton of bricks, but it hadn't. Had he any reason to be mad? Besides, when she had slept with Velvet, she wouldn't have even known if he was still alive, let alone capable of remembering or reuniting their previous flame. The news made him realize that the moral fiber of Cadence Whitaker was cut from a much more resilient cloth than the fabric of his own moral code.

She was a better person. Period.

And the fact she had slept with another woman, rather than a man, also made it easier to deal with emotionally. After all, he couldn't compete with Velvet if he wanted to. He didn't have the parts, for one.

Velvet leaned over, kissed him on the cheek and stood up, smiling. She slid the coffee table off the small multi-colored throw rug in front of the fire and laid down on her back staring at him. She set her wine down, peeled off her t-shirt, pulled off her bra, propped herself on one elbow and seductively took a sip of wine, her beautiful breasts exposed, the nipples growing erect. "What are you waiting for?" she said. "We don't know how long we're going to live."

Nathan thought somehow this seemed the right thing to do. He remembered how Cadence had smiled erotically when Velvet had, jokingly or not he didn't know, suggested a threesome. What a perfect way to remember Cadence. By making love to the woman who made love to her, perhaps even loved her like he did. They could solidify their mutual affection for Cadence by making love with each other.

Or, at least that's how he rationalized it as he quickly grabbed a small comforter from a linen closet, stripped off his clothes, joined Velvet and began kissing her face, fondling her inviting breasts, becoming one with her desirable body, losing himself in the tantalizingly pleasurable sensations of the moment.

Who knows how long I'm going to live.

Chapter Twenty-One

"Shut your fucking mouth if you want to live," Velvet whispered, standing over his bed, her index finger to her mouth.

After their night of carnal pleasure, Velvet had disappeared to an upper bedroom and Nathan, after contemplating the night's passion, trying to determine if there was more to it than a one-night stand for Velvet, had finally grabbed an oil lantern and made his way up to one of the empty bedrooms on the second floor and fallen asleep in one of the spare beds.

She had woken him up in the middle of the night, at least now they could tell it was night, and he had groaned loudly, a ritual since becoming a survivor of a nuclear disaster.

Seeing the seriousness in her eyes, the AK-47 in her hands, he slowly got up, wiped the sleep from his eyes, grabbed his weapon and flashlight, quickly dressed, and followed her down the hallway.

A floorboard creaked and they both stopped. Velvet pointed to the front door and whispered, "I heard something move outside."

They looked down the stairs at the front door. It jerked open and a deformed man, thin gray hair, crazed expression, tumors the size of grapefruits growing from his head and neck, took one step inside the house, growled, and was riddled with bullets from the jury-rigged machine gun.

He groaned, jerked spasmodically, as gunshot riddled his chest and head, dropped to the floor and died as the machine gun continued firing until the magazine was spent.

Velvet rushed down the stairs, stood beside the door motioning for Nathan to follow. As the mutant bled out on the floor, they shone flashlight beams outside into the darkness and listened. The night was silent.

"Give me a hand," Velvet said, pulling open the door, grabbing the corpse by one foot. Nathan grabbed the other and they pulled him outside, his dead head thumping on the steps as they descended the small porch into the darkness.

"Do you hear anything?" Velvet asked, after a minute.

"No, do you?"

"I thought I heard a faint crying from over there." She pointed up a hill, where the moon shone orange in the distance.

Nathan listened, heard nothing. He shook his head, then stopped, his eyes widening. He could hear a crying sound, almost like a chant, off in the distance, seemingly from the other side of the hill.

"Shit, we better get inside," he said.

They scrambled up the steps and locked the bullet-riddled wooden door. Nathan rushed into the basement, a small damp crawl space, looking for some tools. A few minutes later, he returned with some wooden boards, two hammers and some nails. He dropped some boards next to Velvet, who was peering out the front door, handed her a hammer and nails, and ran to the back door.

She had already locked it, so he hammered a few boards up for extra security.

They ran upstairs, each occupying a separate bedroom, opened the windows, trained their respective firearms outside and waited.

The wailing, in unison now, grew louder.

Then they saw the lights. Each of the mutants carried flaming torches, walking purposefully toward the front of the house. There were twelve, maybe fifteen in total, now coming toward them, perhaps a hundred yards from the property.

"Take them out," Velvet ordered and shots rang out. She methodically focused the laser sight from the high-powered rifle on individual foreheads, pop, pop, pop, and mutants dropped dead, brain matter splattering out the backs of their heads.

Nathan mowed them down with his AK-47, watching them stumble and drop dead as the bullets penetrated. Carrying the torches, they were very visible, easy targets.

"Nine dead," Velvet yelled from the other bedroom while reloading. "Six more to go."

"Five," Nathan said, spraying bullets across the head and chest of a mutant who had started jogging toward the house. Do zombies run?

"Something's wrong," Velvet said as she blew the brains out of another one that had begun charging toward the small house. "I'm going downstairs. We can't let them get close with those torches. This place will go up like a tinder box. Hold them off." She ran down the stairs, smashed the glass of the bay window with her rifle, strung it back over her shoulder and pulled the AK-47 off the other shoulder. At this closer range, the enemy within fifty feet, she preferred the rapid fire of the machine gun.

Nathan turned his head for a second as she disappeared and quickly began firing. *But there was a mutant to my left. Where is he? Where the fuck is he?*

"Velvet," he yelled, his voice now verging on panic. "One got away from me, check the side of the hou ..." He didn't get to finish his sentence as he heard a loud crash below, glanced down the stairs and saw a flaming mutant wrestling with Velvet, her hair now on fire.

Go down or shoot the mutants here ... go down or shoot the mutants here ... shoot them first and go down.

He pointed the machine gun nozzle out the window and killed the last two mutants, by now a few feet from the front door. One chucked a flaming torch into the shattered bay window as he dropped dead. By the time he raced down the stairs, the living room was a wall of flame and he could barely see two figures engaged in battle, blood-curdling screams echoing from the fiery hell.

He tried to step into the room but the flame whooshed out and attacked him, igniting his parka. He hit the hallway floor rolling, finally managing to put out the flames but not before the nylon fabric burned into his skin on both forearms. Standing up, he also smelled burning hair and frantically smacked his head, extinguishing the flames and burning his hands.

Being chased by the rapidly advancing wall of fire, Nathan ran down the hallway, crashing into the back door, smashing it open, landing on the porch and rolling off onto a rock surface. His pants on fire—he tapped the flames out and winced, slowly standing and backing away. The house exploded, punctuated by a huge fireball that leaped up, licking at the night sky, a shower of debris falling everywhere.

Along with the dead body of the only friend I had left in this world.

Chapter Twenty-Two

"What kind of crazy fucked up world do we live in?" Nathan said weakly, stretched out on the deck of *Delilah Blue* ten days later, as it tossed in rough waters in the hot afternoon sun. After the explosion he had narrowly escaped with his life, scrambling down the rocky path, falling, getting up, falling again, until he finally made it, cut, bruised, and battered, to the boat, fired it up and pulled away from shore, the evening sky lit up by the fire and by a procession of torches, held by mutants, slowly following him to the Atlantic Ocean.

He was now out of fuel, food, water and ammo after spending the last few rounds fending off an attack of mutant birds. Tired of the struggle, no longer possessing the will to live, he waited for his death, embraced and welcomed it. His throat was parched, his skin blistering from the hot sun. He stared up into the orange sky, too weak to move another muscle, and felt the life force draining from his body.

The letter to Melissa James, her father's last wish, would never arrive. If she was even alive, she would never know how much her father really loved her. And Nathan would not be given an opportunity to change and become a better person. But, he didn't care anymore as the difficult journey had taught him the importance of love and how trivial our obsessions with material possessions, petty little financial worries, are in comparison to the meaning of the deep bonds we form in our lives.

Would he ever be remembered by his journalistic prowess, by his ability to purchase four rental properties, buy a house, a nice car, even a motorcycle? He doubted it. He thought the only thing he would be remembered for would be the bonds of love he had formed and the strength of those bonds. And, if during this journey, he had managed to influence people in a positive way, change the direction of their lives for the better, than he supposed he would also be remembered for that.

But his memory still wasn't firing on all cylinders and he had only a vague recollection of doing anything remotely charitable. For the most part, like many other people he supposed, his life had been a journey of self-obsession and absorption. But he did remember volunteering at a senior's facility, reading to the elderly, playing chess, talking to them, taking them on the odd outing. And, other than his relationship with Cadence, his friends and family, and he now counted Velvet among that small group, the volunteer effort had filled his life with a meaning and purpose he had not thought possible.

Talking to the elderly, people who had been so popular in their younger years, and for some reason largely abandoned by family and friends as they grew old, had been as therapeutic for Nathan as talking to a shrink. He put smiles on their faces and they gave his life meaning and purpose. And made him happy, something that many people strive for in their lives but few manage to attain.

He felt his vision slowly blurring, his thoughts becoming disconnected and unfocused. He closed his eyes and orange turned to black. *I'm going to die now.* He smiled—the monumental struggle finally over. He would finally find the inner peace he had searched for his entire life.

He listened to his heart: Bup ... bup ... bup ... bup ....
bup .... bup.

Chapter Twenty-Three

Bup-bup-bup—wop-wop-wop—bup-bup-bup—wop-wop-wop, the chopper rotors echoed in the silent sky as Canadian military co-pilot Jeff Anderson pointed to a small white dot in the middle of the Atlantic Ocean. Young, clean cut and eager to impress pilot and commander Randall Stiessman, his trainer and mentor, he wanted to make sure they returned to base from this sortie with a few survivors, ones who hadn't been contaminated by radiation and exposed to the deadly virus, unleashed by the smart bomb that had dropped following the nuclear bombs. Those responsible wanted to be sure those not killed by radiation exposure or the devastation from the initial blast, were eventually infected and killed by the subsequent biological weapon.

What they hadn't anticipated was a few people's immune systems had built-in defense mechanisms for the virus. If they weren't infected now, five months after the blast, military scientists discovered they wouldn't be infected.

"Over there," Jeff said. "It looks like a boat."

Randall nodded, steering the helicopter closer to get a better view. "You said that last time and it was a whitecap wave."

Jeff peered through the binoculars again while three soldiers sitting in the back readied their weapons. "No, that's definitely a boat. And there's someone on it."

"Probably dead or infected," Randall said. So far all of the sorties to the island of Newfoundland had involved killing crazed mutants. They had yet to find a single sane survivor.

"Stay frosty men," he said, lowering the craft to within thirty feet above the boat.

"Should we go down and see if he's alive?" Jeff asked.

"Your success rate hasn't been that good lately," Randall said, smiling. "You're nothing more than a glorified mutant detector."

"Well, we won't know until we try?" Jeff said.

Randall was about to abort the mission and fly away, when for reasons he didn't understand, he suddenly changed his mind and nodded back at the men. "Open the hatch and take the rope down, Stan," he ordered one of them.

Stan Imes, the medical doctor on board, popped the hatch open, dropped the rope and expertly slid down, landing on deck beside Nathan, while Randall steadied the chopper. Stan knelt down, checked Nathan's vitals, pressed a button on his two-way radio and said, "He's alive, commander, but just barely. And he doesn't show any signs of infection."

Jeff grinned. "My first survivor."

A few minutes later, Nathan leaned against the window of the chopper after being infused with an IV and drinking at least a gallon of water. The three soldiers eyed him curiously as he looked out at the barren landscape of The Rock.

It was an effort for him to speak, but he finally managed. "Where we going anyway?"

"We have a ship a few miles the other side of The Rock," Stan said. "You'll be quarantined for a month, just as a precaution."

He had lots more questions but didn't have the strength for them now. He was content to gaze down at the devastation as it passed before his weary eyes.

"Any other survivors that you know about?" Stan asked.

"No," Nathan said, not bothering to mention the Neanderthals. *Let those fuckers fend for themselves. Never mind that. Let them rot in fucking hell on Earth.*

But then Nathan saw someone below, hidden behind a makeshift rock fortress, shooting attacking mutants with a rifle. There were hundreds of them and it wouldn't be long before the survivor, whoever it was, would be overrun and killed.

"Down there," Nathan said, pointing.

Jeff immediately pulled the binoculars out and nodded excitedly. "That's two," he said. "Bring it over there, commander."

The chopper got closer, the hatch popped open and the soldiers began firing on the mutants, who were dropping like flies under heavy machine gun fire. The woman below waved as they neared and a rope was lowered.

With seconds to spare, she grabbed it as mutant hands pawed at her legs, trying to pry her loose. One grabbed on and was airborne with her momentarily, but she delivered a hard kick to its head and the mutant fell to its death.

The chopper accelerated into the sky as the mechanical rope was reeled in. Two soldiers grabbed her arms as she neared the hatch and pulled her in, closing the door behind her. They helped her into a seat.

She panted as she caught her breath. "Thanks. You couldn't have come at a better time."

Nathan stared at the woman and his mouth dropped. Half of her hair had been burned off and the new hairdo resembled a half-completed Mohawk cut. He felt the adrenaline rushing through his veins, infusing him with a sudden energy he didn't know was possible considering his condition. "Velvet," he said. "You're alive."

She instantly recognized him and rushed over, wrapping him in a bear hug and planting a wet kiss on his lips.

The soldiers whistled and laughed.

"How did you survive?" Nathan asked.

"As soon as the fire broke out, I hid in the basement. After the house burned to the ground, I crawled out of the rubble. Life hasn't been easy lately."

"No doubt," Nathan said. "But now we have a second chance."

As the chopper thumped along, heading farther out into the ocean, the carnage on Newfoundland shrinking as it faded into the distance, Nathan still had a few anxious thoughts tugging at his mind, swirling around, demanding attention. *If we do have a second chance, what kind of life will it be? Does humankind... do we, have the capacity and intelligence to learn from our mistakes, to not repeat the same mistakes over and over again?*

He wasn't sure.

But he doubted it.

Also by William Blackwell

Phantom Rage, Poison Rage, Infected Rage
Nightmare's Edge
Resurrection Point
Brainstorm
Rule 14
Assaulted Souls
Assaulted Souls II
Assaulted Souls III
Blood Curse
Black Dawn
The Strap
The End is Nigh
Orgon Conclusion
Freaky Franky
The Witch's Tombstone
The Dark Menace
Tales of Damnation
In Your Dreams
Macabre Alley
A Head for an Eye

Assaulted Souls II Preview

"Love this series. Give it a try." -Amazon

"I highly recommend this series to anyone that is looking for a high octane, action-packed book." -For the Novel Lovers blog

Clinging to life, two post-apocalyptic disaster survivors are rescued from a chaotic and violent struggle on the East Coast of Canada. Believing they're safe, they are precipitously quarantined on a ship by the government, watched 24/7, and poked and prodded like laboratory animals.

Nathan King is assured by chemical biologist Stan Imes that the injections are merely anti-radiation medication, and the quarantine is necessary to insure they aren't infected by a rage virus that has turned much of the population into killer zombies.

But survivor Velvet Jones doesn't buy it. After learning of a vicious murder, she tries to convince Nathan they are being genetically modified into the perfect super soldiers to fight the battles of the demented megalomaniacs in power.

Nathan isn't so sure. But he soon realizes his mind is not his own anymore after violent impulses surface, propelling him to want to murder Velvet, perhaps his only ally in this living hell.

Soon he learns they aren't alone. Other test subjects, some whose blood types spawn uncontrollable violent urges, are kept in a secret facility and subjected to all manner of torturous behavior control techniques. The so-called deviants are ultimately executed if their so-called adverse behaviors cannot be rectified.

Suffering violent and murderous side effects, Nathan and Velvet must find some sanity in a world gone mad, and fight the most horrifying battle of their lives.

About the Author

Canadian dark fiction author William Blackwell studied journalism at Mount Royal University and English literature at The University of British Columbia. He worked as a journalist and a newspaper editor for many years before pursuing his passion for storytelling. His novels have been characterized as graphic, edgy, and at times terrifying. Currently living on a secluded acreage on Prince Edward Island, Blackwell finds much of his inspiration from Mother Nature, odd people, traveling, and bizarre nightmares.

Author Comments

Thank you for reading this book. I would be eternally grateful if you would post a book review on your favorite book retailer website. A positive review is the highest compliment a writer can receive. Reviews are crucial to the success of any author and also help readers find books. You don't have to say much. A few sentences will suffice.

In other news, I have a gift for you. Complete the signup form below with your name and email address and download a FREE copy of *Resurrection Point*, a dark tale about the horrifying consequences of experimenting with death and resurrection. You'll be kept up to date on blog posts, new releases, and freebies. I promise I won't spam you and you can unsubscribe at any time.

Thanks again for your support.

http://www.wblackwell.com/free-ebook/